Mia

by Kayla Eason

For Nana

i

Night dismantles. Sky peels back, revealing nothing and everything. Crepe, sulfur lit breeze warps familiarity with the earth. Mia dips into the lassitude, stretching her hand forward, the touch welding to his breath. She listens, her palm to Sebastian's spine as he sleeps. Blood concentrating, the sound of velvet.

Mia has been in foster care with Sebastian and his mother, Val, for four years. She has known him most of her life. His warmth in her hand is a shaving of the night, every night. It is a color. Midnight, charcoal blue and sensitive.

Mia can't remember ever falling asleep easily; though only months prior, when she was still ten years old, she would drift off unknowingly. She dreamt of her mother's desert scent, the purple fragrance of her breath, her lightning blonde hair. Her mother stroking Mia's back. Or she dreamt of Sebastian's hands, sweat—iron rivers in the creases of his palms. Monkey bars. An empty playground. Dirt, sun, soundless metals.

Mia stares at the yard, a formless dark. Age eleven is a precipice. Night has become an introspective space where her thoughts flow from one another, return, braid. Some nights she enjoys feeling detached from all things—feeling as if she and Sebastian hang alone above a vague life. And other nights, she wishes Sebastian was still awake so that they could talk, maybe play *would you rather*—would you rather have a million dollars or see the future? Fly or have the ability to read a person's thoughts? Be alive now, or in a different time? Become a rock, moveable, or a mountain? Eat a dead fish or a pound of sand? The fish baked in sun, gel piecing off its needled form, or to feel sand claying within organs, element weight marring flexibility.

Mia breathes forward, and her mind dispels ribbons, the sky. Her fingers slip across Sebastian's skin; her thoughts bend around him, lock into his warmth. She closes her eyes, and then she's pressed into her mother's body like an imprint, bruise-colored. She's clay. She's dreaming of a hug. She's a sleeping child.

Sometime, in the future, Mia will have already started to forget.

A Saturday morning:

Mia is five, sandwiched between her sleeping parents. Six a.m., unripe sky. The Salton Sea yellows two miles away. Sulfur crystals tint the shore. Mia twists sweat from her creases, her legs slipping against her mother's, her feet pushing against her father's calves. Hunger wakes her, and then the alarm clock sounds.

Air clots in the studio apartment and already the temperature has reached the 80s outside. Mia's cheeks are scarlet. Her father rolls from bed, turns to cup her face.

You got sleep in your eyes, Mia, her father says. Putty voice, he smiles.

He washes his face in the kitchen sink with dish soap, then mixes a cup of instant coffee. Her mother rises from the sheets, thighs dimpled and slick. She kisses Mia on the face, pressing her lips against her forehead until Mia lays back giggling, then her mother kisses Mia's stomach and her knees.

Daddy's first day at the new job, her mother says.

Mia's father sits on the bed to drink his coffee, and Mia slips under his arm to hug his belly. With a loose fist, she rubs her eyes and forehead, her skin tender with the sticky air.

My legs are longer than your legs, her father says.

When I'm grown-up, I'll be tallest on earth, Mia says.

Gonna hit your head on a star.

Mia watches her mother cook in her underwear. Oil sizzles, snapping. Her mother slides three chunks of hamburger into a pan. In a white cloud, grease billows fleshy. The meat bubbles, scent thickening, nearing viscous quality. Mia is starving, but knows better than to ask for something to eat while the hamburger cooks. Her stomach feels like a hole. She could fit sun break in the hole, the sea, gallons of sea. She could fit summer, all of the cracked earth and quiet. Space, gaping. A vinegar feeling. A taut feeling. Mia smells flesh whitening to brown.

Her father's sweat mingles with her own. Heat paints, sloppy. She opens her mouth to speak, beg for a piece of toast, though she knows her mother will not allow it—*it's the end of the month, we need to get through the weekend. This is a special day, special breakfast.*

The hole widens. Burning fat sinks in.

And that's when she hears the rain.

Turning her head, she sees only sun beyond the window. No rain, but tiny beats, circular cadence, and she swears the sound emanates near her body, or from her body.

What's that? Her father hears it too.

Her mother peers out the window, spatula limp in her hand.

I feel real nervous, her father says.

Mia looks over him—the ceiling moves above his head. Tubular pattern, inky black in glints, marbled brown. Her father squints at her, confused. Mia's eyes grow, attempting to make sense of the movement and now, she notices, the moving walls too. The marbled texture spreads up the far wall behind her father the way fire spreads across a plain: unruly, ingesting, but slow.

Mia?

Her name is wrapped in the heat. Her name comes from inside the hole.

The house is alive. She points to the moving wall.

In unison her parents look to find the texture feathering upward to the ceiling where the mass had begun to disperse. A storm, Mia thinks. The sound of rain.

Roaches, her father says, and Mia's mother screams.

Oil voluptuous, smoke suffocating.

Her father shoves his hands beneath Mia's armpits, and hoists her toward the door while hundreds of cockroaches crawl toward the cooking meat. Mia's scream is a higher pitch than her mother's, but her father laughs with depth, his face gleaning.

What you got, God? Her father says. Throw it at me, got the best damn sense of humor under your sun.

Outside the apartment, dry heat lighting up asphalt, cloudless sky now a crystal piece. Her father is bent laughing, and her mother stands pant-less still clutching the spatula. What the hell? What in the hell? She shouts.

Mia slips her hands beneath her shirt. Her sweat cold. She thinks she can feel her stomach moving. Pressing down, she imagines she is pregnant, a living thing kicking within her. She's seen a pregnant belly
before, knows how heavy and full a woman appears. But Mia feels only empty.

Orchestral: the insects and hunger, feverish temperatures. Mia wants breakfast. She wants a fan. She wants to bathe, wring the scent of fat from her hair. Her small body compounds all of these desires to tears, inflexible and fast. She is full of what she sees. Tiny legs sticking to her walls. There is no blood.

Later, after her father goes to work, and after their neighbor helps her mother spray pesticide, set sticky traps, and months later, when her father loses that job, as Mia lies between her mother and father one night, her eyes still watching the ceiling for movement, her parents' bodies sickly aromatic, limp and intoxicated, sleeping like the dead, there is real rain, transcendent in the dark.

She listens carefully. Drops tap desert, then swell from millions into a singular, long exhale. She had misremembered the sound of rain.

It's nothing like hunger.

Sebastian breathes.

And Mia listens.

The surrounding desert of Marina Sal gapes like a hole in the throat. In the distance, black-necked stilts husk dead tilapia on the Salton Sea's shore, the sound an echo across still, viscous water. Sebastian's shirtless chest radiates heat, which Mia can smell, his salt as downy as the crepe petals of Matilija poppies—those white flowers growing in the yard, softening the June night. During late hours, the Southern California desert is a violet, slow composed thing.

Mia and Sebastian lie side by side on a browned mattress on the back patio, a cracked concrete square ebbed by yellow grass. It's where they sleep each summer. Mia lies on her back and stares at the sky. Sebastian lies on his back, too, hands across his stomach, loose and soft from having quickly lost baby weight. At eleven, Mia is changing too, rounding out in her chest and thighs, hips opening. She senses a stress to her body freely moving; feels her parts like pieces she attaches each morning, a body suit wired with nerve lights.

Boys at school have been quick to point out how her breasts jerk when she runs. One afternoon during recess, Mia was playing freeze tag. Benny had grabbed at her shirt tail to tag her, and her body jolted mid-leap. He'd laughed, your tits are still moving!

Lucy, Mia's closest girlfriend since preschool and youngest of three daughters, told her to ask Val about bras, so she did. When Val took Mia to Walmart, Mia acquired her first bra. An A-cup, no padding, the soft cotton milk-colored.

Her thigh gently presses against the side of Sebastian's thigh, which is warm through jersey shorts. Lately, she's come to rely on his body being near. Last Saturday night the temperature cooled to 89 degrees. The two changed into their bathing suits. The moon ascended through heat. In the driveway, they doused their bodies with copper-scented water from the hose. Fat moths convulsed around the bulb dangling low in the garage. Sebastian pressed his thumb into the water stream, spraying Mia. Screaming, she tried to pry the hose from his hands and during the wrestle, she realized suddenly, like identifying a word on the tip of the tongue, that his hand gripped her hip. His stomach against her own. She liked the physicality. Through him, an awareness of her own body and how their bodies felt together. A study of nature, shapes of movement. Feeling the sun in her bones, or flower petals melting into the palm The feeling of him spatial in her chest. A temperature in her mind.

Closeness, the intrinsic awareness of his touch, has become necessary, and since that night Mia can't fall asleep unless her leg touches Sebastian's leg or her arm touches his arm. Nights when the two are lying back to back, spines zipped, she sleeps deeply.

Flowers sweat against the night. Heat between their bodies. Heat ballooning the sky. Mia sighs. Like her body, these feelings do not seem her own. She hasn't before ruminated on touch, hasn't before felt so comforted by the warmth of another person. Not in this way, in that she wants to meld with Sebastian, to feel what he feels.

They have shared the mattress every summer for the four years she has lived with him. With no sheets, the padding beneath their backs smells like their bodies, perspiration and dust sticking to the smoothness behind their knees. All the nights together bleed into a single feeling for Mia: paralysis-like, one long, stretching moment that she'd choose to inhabit over any other time. His thigh warm. His breathing a rhythm which has, into so many evening hours, carried her to sleep. Sometimes she'll wake and her chest breaks open. In a dream, Sebastian wasn't there. He wasn't beside her, wasn't where he said he would be. Mia would dream that he had left and would never return.

What's the first thing you can remember? Like, as a baby, Mia asks Sebastian.

It's a question she heard once asked on TV. Mia had been watching soaps with Val on a Sunday afternoon. A couple had been lying in bed, comforter pulled just over their naked chests. The man held the woman against him. She was smiling. She told him that she wanted to know everything about him. Details of his childhood, intimate memories. Unhurried, back and forth, the woman's hand stroking the man's chest.

Sebastian is silent. In thought, he reaches out and touches a memory. There is the Mickey Mouse wallpaper in his bedroom. Though, maybe there's a memory earlier than that. His mother's hair. Or a vision of the front yard, dead grass, a batman action figure used to hammer red ants. No, it must be the hallway in the house. The brown carpet. Light through the window at the end of the hall a cloud of silver. Something about this memory feels old, as if it didn't come from a picture, from a story, but a first glimpse of awareness.

He says he thinks he can remember crawling down the hall. He says, I can see the back window like I was looking at it from the ground. I think that's the first thing I can remember. He mindlessly pinches his belly. The TV from Val's room glows through the window and in its silver light, Mia can see Sebastian's stretch marks. The scars are faint, shiny, drawn across the ball of his shoulder. The muscle of his bicep is slightly plump, and as Mia studies his scars and arms, she touches her own shoulders with barely-there fingertips.

Sebastian does not often think about the past. He knows what he likes: skateboarding wild and fluid, the adrenaline of action movies, and comics, staying up late in his bedroom when the whole house is asleep. He doesn't allow his mind to wander far; it's easier this way. Sebastian has learned to limit the distance his thoughts travel.

Sebastian does like Mia's company. Though he doesn't consider her an actual sister, he doesn't acknowledge that she is anything else in relation to him. She doesn't have freckles like Lora in the eighth grade. Mia doesn't wear bracelets like Mary from class, bracelets which collect on her wrists, chunky beads a textured mass that shines when she raises her hand. Mia is the person who sometimes wears his pajamas, who sleeps beside him at night, who receives the same kind of socks on Christmas. Mia is family. She is always around, and she always has been.

I know mine, Mia says, voice rising. She points at the two cigarette burn scars on her face—circular and pink. One in the center of her forehead and one on her right cheek. When my dad did this.

You don't really remember that, do you? Sebastian props himself on one elbow.

Mia nods. The memory moves in her periphery the way a person imagines shadows. It takes shape and twists into a whirlwind spinning in the sand. She feels a kind of spinning when she thinks about the back of her neck gripped in her father's hand, and being tugged into his breath. How he hissed through clamped teeth, saliva bubbling in the corners of his mouth. Mia was three, maybe four years old when he burned her. His words grating against neck cords, *Shut up—Shut up—Shut up*. He'd reached for the cigarette set in the ashtray beside his chair. The T.V. on mute, the crooked ceiling fan squeaking. She didn't see the cigarette descend the air, pinched in her father's fingertips. Heat indistinctly icy and searing in the center of her forehead. Then pressed into her right cheek, here the eye of a wind tunnel, a fleeting rip of clarity in the turning: foreignness. She didn't understand anything concrete about the moment, remembers thinking, *who is this*? How it couldn't be him, but it had been. Heard the paper rip as he'd sucked ash, red eyes looking beyond her.

And the whirlwind dying on his dead cigarette.

What did it feel like?

Sebastian's head lies tilted on his propped shoulder, gaze downturned to her face. The dark's euphony slows her gaze, a shallow wave upon wave whisper. She feels embarrassed for looking at him so straight on. She wants to step from her body, to understand how her body crawls when she does not move a muscle, to hold the quality of eyes that look at her.

What did it feel like? He asks again.

So hot that it was cold.

You really remember it?

Maybe I made it up and just think it. I got the scars somehow. But I know he had me by the back of the neck. I know that really happened.

Sebastian slips his hand beneath her neck and his palm, his fingers, are warm.

Like that?

She nods. He doesn't speak, but in the silver light she watches as he squints, the severe furrow of his brows. He clears his throat.

Mia wonders—is this what it's like to be married?

To be touched softly, to be worried about.

In the morning, Mia wakes on the patio mattress to a glazed desert. She rises silently, trying not to wake Sebastian. His mouth open, drooling. She smiles, rubbing her eyes of sleep. For a moment she watches the way his fingers curl in dream.

Val curls her hair in front of the living room television. Sun just rising—an orange in purple air. Dust spins through spears of light in the living room. Wood-paneled walls turning golden.

Mia locks herself in the bathroom. It's the last day of school, early June. Temperatures will reach 110 degrees in Marina Sal by the afternoon. She unfolds an elastic-lined cotton bra and knee-length dress, and holds them one at a time to the yellow vanity lighting. The dress is short-sleeved, rose-colored. The crisp white bra has triangular pads to hug her chest.

She takes off her pajamas, folds them neatly, and turns to examine her body in the full-length mirror. Shifting her weight from hip to hip, she watches her breasts move as her body moves. She cups them in two hands like a push-up bra, imitating the way she had seen Val's swell with under-padding. Mia is still trying to embrace this excess flesh that has only recently developed. Dimpled softness packed on her stomach and thighs. Val said that many girls undergo puberty around eleven or twelve, that their bodies change and they feel new things. Mia finds herself sometimes squeezing the new softness of her body, releasing tension that stiffens in her hands. She's often frustrated by how kids at school seem more interested in looking at each other now. A boy tells her to wear a bra. A boy tells her to suck it in. A boy tells her that her skirt is too short. Before the past year, Mia had never been so occupied with her appearance. The siege is new; the rules she's desperate to learn. And when she looks at herself in the mirror, she wishes her naked body and the changes away.

There's a pound at the door.

Mia, I have to pee, Sebastian says.

Hold on!

She slips the bra over her head and sticks out her chest to eye the new shape. Then she steps into the dress, brushes her brown hair, and tucks her head toward her neck, smiling with closed lips. She tries smiling with teeth, but doesn't like this as much. Her bottom teeth tilt to the right and the veneer is peeling away, leaving brown, cloudy marks on the two false teeth. When Mia was three years old, she had to have silver caps applied to her two front teeth due to rotting. The silver caps had been replaced with two false teeth by age five, but the quality of dental work proved poor over the last seven years. Mia closes her lips, smiles again at this girl who looks taller than she remembers being, whose heart-shaped face looks plumper in her cheeks, and lashes darker somehow. Shadows growing from her new features, creating new depth. Flesh folding where it once had not. The touching of her thighs.

Mia, I got to pee.

Opening the door, she finds Sebastian with arms folded. His sleepy eyes opening. He wears an oversized t-shirt with holes along the seams.

You took forever, he says.

You look little in that shirt, she says.

Come on, move!

His hand presses against her shoulder. Mia walks down the hallway. Brown carpet crunching beneath her bare feet. She runs her fingers along peeling wallpaper.

Val sits at the kitchen table, smoking a cigarette and listening to the news on the TV. Mia sits and pours herself a bowl of Captain Crunch.

The house, which Val has rented for fourteen years, is half-trailer, half built-on. The kitchen is part of the original trailer. Compact with caramel wood panels curving from wall to ceiling. The table is a booth attached to the wall, and the turquoise-colored seats are tearing from years of sitting.

Mia catches words from the television in the living room directly across from the kitchen. The news reports a plane crashed in the Atlantic, a flight from Los Angeles to Australia. Mia doesn't listen too carefully to the details of the report, but hears the anchor say, *The pilot's last words were 'We're dead,'* and in her mind, Mia can see the ocean's blue sucking the plane down from clouds. She imagines Australia to be a withdrawn nest of strange animals. She's just barely able to understand the terror of drowning, the ocean a vacuum. Dying is to never return, but to go somewhere mysterious. How far to the bottom of the world? The darkest blue. Black. The plane falls into space, the ocean. Both an endless thing. The expansiveness of both is the way dying must feel.

Damn, Val says, dragging the cigarette, then releases smoke the full capacity of her lungs. In the mornings, Val rarely speaks. She wears her boxy post office uniform and listens to the news on the television. Her face hollow, cherry-wood eyes rich against her complexion, eyes lined black. She draws on fine brows, plasters curls with Ultra-Strength hairspray, smears shimmering lotion on her legs so they shine in the sun.

Val looks at Mia's soft hair brushed, her face in the morning light. A memory comes: Mia and Sebastian are babies. Val's mother is still alive, and Mia's mother is there.

They are all five in the car driving to a Planned Parenthood in San Bernardino. Mia's mother had needed stiches after giving birth to Mia, and two months later, her vagina was still tender and bleeding.

At a gas station, a haloed sun scaling the chalky morning, Val's mother turns and snaps a photo of Val and Mia's mother nursing their newborns in the back seat. Mia and Sebastian making small fists reaching toward each of their mothers' chins. The picture is still framed in Val's room.

Mia sits before her and Val misses Mia simply because she's growing older. Val moves farther away from new motherhood. Mia and Sebastian move farther away from infancy. For a moment, Val longs for the newness, the pivotal first few months after she gave birth to Sebastian. No stretch of time has since felt as fresh with possibility. That morning was years ago and Val feels as old as she'll ever grow. She has felt this way for a long time.

Sebastian appears in the kitchen. He's combed his brown hair to the side, as he always does, and has just popped several pimples, leaving pock marks and blood specs on his round chin. Mia pours him a bowl of cereal. She sits back and crosses her legs. The skirt shifts above her birth mark. Her eyes flick up to see if he sees her leg, the mark.

Sebastian breathes through his nose as he chews, milk bubbling in the corners of his mouth, eyes half-closed on the wall beyond Mia. She cannot see his hand on his knee beneath the table, but he's tracing a large scab, like cement to his fingertip, remembering the fall he took on his board when skating across Bay Street in the dark. He had hit broken glass. The board faltering for only a moment, his body bending forward without restraint into a black hole second, spit out sliding across gravel.

There had been a lot of blood, and his leg was still stiff, knee cap purple. He anticipates the scar with satisfaction. He doesn't notice the supple brightness of Mia's expression, or how her legs are crossed toward him.

You'll be late, Val says. Get going. I didn't get to buying bread, so there aren't sandwiches today. I got you each a Coke though, and there's still some Fruit Roll-Ups.

We get pizza, Sebastian says. Ms. Villa is getting cheese kind and pepperoni kind.

Good, Val says. Do your dishes before you leave, please. Have lots of fun on the last day, alright?

Mia cleans the dishes while Sebastian ties his shoes, all-white Vans high-tops, a prized possession. After school, Sebastian will skateboard with his friends. They skate empty pools at deserted resorts or houses. The bowl-shape yawning deep, covered in graffiti and with even, lip-curled edges. The graffiti acts as a poem to the blood, words blurring in their vision as they sail the concrete:

DE LA LUNA, LAS MANOS.
CANT FUCK 4 FREE.
BUKOWSKI.
HAIL METH SMOKE GOD.

APPLAUD.

ABANDON.

QUESTION.

Sebastian likes to balance, to lean into the force which ignites him forward. He admires his shoes, imagining the soles pressing into the board, wheels grinding, in his wake parting the words, the colors. One more day of school and he's free, and he can think about less, catch the wind, move more. And with more movement, his body will loosen into the long hours, afternoons which last days. Nowhere to go, and all the unquenchable therein.

As they leave for school, Sebastian holds the door for Mia, and they step out to walk a dusty street, desert bleached around them. They pass an old miniature golf course, where a decomposing castle and T-Rex and windmill sag. They pass a diner, still operating, where the newspaper dispensers haven't been filled in years, and the same expressionless people drinking hot coffee in weather too hot for it. They pass a building which had once provided tourist information, but is now covered in graffiti and paintings: grey cityscape, VW Bug with spider legs, and a bony Jesus wearing a red bikini.

Someone had painted a woman on the building too, with curving features and long, dark hair. Her face turned down, kissing a small cactus in her hands. Her feet painted red as if bleeding. She is naked, and each time Mia passes the woman, she notices the way the body is the only soft shape against the flat, geometric composition of the desert.

Mia sweats, staining the chest of her dress with downturned U-shapes. Her thighs chafing. She can smell her own body—the oils of her skin and creamy perfume of soap. Her hair gluing itself to her cheeks and forehead.

She sees sweat gather in beads on the back of Sebastian's neck. She reaches out a finger and touches the moisture.

You sweat more than me.

He swats her hand away. Don't, he says, drawing out the word.

She skips forward and turns to face him, smiling. In that moment, she doesn't remember the brown marks on her teeth. His gaze draws across her face to her eyes, and their movement slows her step, working like music, decelerating time. A slow-motion exchange—of what?

They look away from one another. What had he been thinking? The sky is blooming cloudless, and she senses his person in relation to her own, affecting her, not just dwelling near her. Mia feels her heart. She feels pretty.

Sebastian kicks pebbles. Mia watches her legs extend forward as she walks, and she hums. When they reach school, Sebastian's friends, Daniel and Benny, are near the wall-ball court.

Hey, Mia, Daniel says, arms crossed over a shirt that's faded and tight. His head's shaved, wet-looking, and a rat-tail snakes around and sticks to the front of his neck.

Mia smiles, nods to him. Her back against the wall; the boys form a half-circle. Standing erect, Mia sucks in her stomach, and the action pushes out her chest. She crosses one leg in front of the other, and listens while the boys talk back and forth until Daniel turns to her.

Why do you smile like that? Daniel says.

Like what? She says.

Without teeth. Is it 'cuz your teeth are fucked up? Daniel bares his teeth, sliding his tongue across them to show their straightness.

Mia tightens her lips, and Daniel laughs.

Sebastian nudges Mia on the shoulder, and nods toward the playground. His touch is felt to the bone. *Remember wishbones?* She wants to ask. That snapping sound. On Thanksgiving, Sebastian couldn't tell her his wish because then it wouldn't come true. His wish had followed her as she walked to school. It had stared at her when she ate. *What did you wish for? Nothing*, he'd say. *I wished for nothing.* But she didn't believe him. She'd imagine that they had made the same wish. She'd imagine that Sebastian would turn to her in the night, whisper, *I love you.* But he never had. She stares at him, and his eyes gesture her away.

Do you like my new bra, Daniel? The question out before Mia realizes what she is asking. The boys look at her.

Mia? Sebastian says.

I got a new bra. It makes my boobs rounder and nice, don't you think? Her voice slips.

Sebastian's head shakes at a glacial pace. Daniel and Benny look at each other, eyebrows screwed with consternation, arms now rigid by their sides.

What's wrong? She says.

Just shut up, Daniel says.

She wants to tell them they are wrong, but she's not sure about what. Wrong to make her feel upset. Wrong to look at her. Her hands itch to push against their bodies, show them that she knows how to press back, lean in, make strain on a moment same as them. She could grab Daniel by the arm and pull him close, speak close to his mouth, *Don't look at me.*

Do you want to see it? She says.

Mia, Sebastian says. No.

She glares at him, and he lifts his hand and touches her arm. She closes her eyes for a beat, feeling angrier than she wants to be, and then walks away. She crosses the playground, hips driving each step. In her mind: heat which pops, or rubs. Drowning in a dream.

She feels their eyes cling to her.

Someone holds her heart in their hand.

This point in time is the landscape.

Desert sand lime in moonlight. Mountains, those lining Arizona and Mexico to the east, sharp fringe. Mountains apricot in the morning, leather mid-day. A pink sea. Sapphire sea. Mirages. People disappearing into earth.

Everything that comes before Mia: a reservoir of gelled moments, the echo of a place, who came and who abandoned, founded and lost. Tried and failed. People and a place which already had happened. Waves of hot light.

A levee breaks in the early 1900s. Water branches from the Colorado river and gushes across lone farmland, a desert bowl, in the Imperial Valley of Southern California. 80,000 gallons of water per second, the Salton Sea accumulates. Irrigation wash-off contributes, mixing rainbow chemicals. Suddenly where earth had thirsted, saline-rich river water inundates, and flooding over 300 miles of low-lying desert, becomes a new sea.

A Las Vegas journalist in the 1930s writes how the baby Salton Sea promises lushness, and people imagine an emergent garden coloring the shores thick with teal fronds, succulents, velvet vegetation. In the '50s and '60s, people from Southern California, Nevada, Arizona, and Northern Mexico migrate to the Salton Sea. They construct resorts, build neighborhoods, grocery stores, schools, post offices. An oasis appears: a glimmering stroke, polished aluminum, greens and blues aglow.

Over the years, saline levels rise higher than that of the Pacific Ocean. Evaporation increases salt deposits. Farm wash-off from cantaloupe, Bermuda grass, sweet onion fields continue to pass into the sea. Speedboats can no longer push through the silver patchwork of dead fish floating atop the surface. Long necks of brown pelican skeletons like dead snakes on the shore. Bones beading mud. Flesh turning to foam. When there is a breeze, it carries an acrid scent, a putrid tightness. Soon, nothing about the water can be trusted. Where parts of the sea recede into air, other parts flood or clot. Colors from the deep earth appear—brilliant pools of pink and milk-gold water. Sulfur laces vaporous balm, dyes the shore the sheen of mercury, bites craters into the land which sparkle as crystal nests.

Communities are abandoned. Whole trailer parks submerged by random flooding. Roads unfinished, cutting off at brush or garbage piles.

The Desert Riviera, The Blue Palm, The Salton Bay Yacht Club, The Chula Vista, one after another, become hollow palaces. All but one school closes. The people who remain have nowhere else to go. Marina Sal expires along with the sea: long, airless spaces between building or person grows more cavernous, emptiness the color of transparency.

In 1975, Mia's maternal grandmother finds a job as a house cleaner after a resort where she had been working shuts down.

She rides a bus thirty-seven miles six days a week from Marina Sal to Indio, where she and three other women meet at an Arco. They pile into one woman's van and clean five or six homes a day throughout Palm Springs. Her grandmother likes the sherbet-colored houses, the open, square rooms airy with sunlight flooding through floor-to-ceiling windows. She doesn't mind climbing a step ladder to clean the windows. She likes looking out at the cacti gardens, the overlay of shadows and cool greens through the glass. She likes to see prickly pear fruit glistening in the mornings, the Koi pond shaded by a dark avocado tree.

One afternoon her grandmother's blood sugar plummets. Being diabetic, she begins to experience chills, grows nauseated. For a small moment, she blacks, hitting her forehead against a marble bathroom counter in a home on Orange Street. Blood collects in her eye lashes. Stitches are needed to sew her left temple. And though she still enjoys the silence of cleaning windows, when she glimpses her own reflection in the polished glass, she sees the scar, she sees the stiffness in her knees, the ache in her lower back, the skin draped beneath her eyes, the routine, the cleaning route, yesterday and years ago and tomorrow.

Her husband had found carpentry work in Calipatria. Each day he drives by alfalfa and sugar beet farms. He bends over blonde wood, saws citrus pine, polishes dust into his lungs. He likes the scent of wood during a strong hot spell. He likes eating a bologna sandwich on his break in the shade of a lebbeck tree, white flower petals falling in spring air. On these lunch breaks, he likes to read a tattered copy of *The Call of the Wild*, the only book he ever enjoys, and imagines what snow tastes like. Imagines solitary wilderness, compact with sterling silence. These afternoons with the earth he treasures. But after years of working with his hands, Mia's grandfather's fingers begin to knot. Wrapping his hand around a beer is painful. His back crinkles into a hook. Standing straight is unnatural, and when his wife reaches out to run a finger over his spine, numbness deletes the touch.

Any other city, even Palm Springs and Calipatria, bleeds into an imprecise dimension of recognition. Marina Sal with its abandoned buildings and homes, overdosed bodies gaseous in the art-deco foyer of the Blue Palm Hotel, elderly who die in their trailers during heat waves, abundant graffiti—EVERYTHING MUST END—junk cars deserted along roads, the scent of molded fish, the sight of a dying sea—these things become all that remain in the world to Mia's grandparents.

In the eighties, those grandparents both die—liver failure for Mia's grandfather, diabetes complications for her grandmother. Mia's mother becomes seventeen and parentless.

At that time Mia's father is squatting in Marina Sal's abandoned Super 8 Motel with a group of families, while picking up random jobs, saving money. He meets Mia's mother at a party in the deserted yacht club's dining room. Her figure curls around him, blurring light and sound through their periphery. He grabs her mother's body in wanting so roughly she's left with green bruises for days.

Her parents are pregnant by eighteen, Mia conceived in an abandoned house. Twilight, beneath graffiti on the ceiling— HEAVEN COME ON MY BODY AND INTO MY HEART.

They live in a small studio apartment in Verano Park, on the south side of the sea, where salt accumulates into sky-blue hills along the shore. Each morning Mia's father travels a half hour to Brawley where he works as a mechanic. He stopped going to school by the fifth grade and has never learned to read, not completely. He values his ability to learn tasks quickly with his hands, though. Likes that the inside of a car is a puzzle, how moving and arranging and screwing parts creates satisfaction—a puzzle he learned through doing, not studying in a book. He likes when his hands makes things move, makes things hot. When he fixes or builds something, when he figures out the steps necessary through an innate understanding within himself, he feels intelligent. He feels in control, creative even.

Six months pregnant, Mia's mother graduates high school and tends their home. In school she had been skilled at Algebra. Her mind working well to intuit the steps in equations, quickly grasping principles of increasing, decreasing, the relation of herself to those who have more than her, those who aren't losing. Her thin hair makes her feel less pretty. She has grey eyes, round cheek bones flushed permanently by rosacea. She likes to pick aloe leaves, smear the juice on sunburns, smell the plastic scent left on her fingertips. Her two favorite songs are Tracy Chapman's "Fast Car" and Janis Joplin's "Piece of My Heart," and both bring tears—an emptying for Chapman, an out-of-body for Joplin.

There are days when Mia's mother lies across an un-made bed, sun pouring over her naked legs, feeling the tight volume and vibrations of her swollen belly, and she feels her heart race, happy to know she will be a mother, and she will count the years, one after another, the accumulation easing the things difficult to put words to. Thoughts spark on desert terrain, lighting a cut of world forgotten.

Three months later, Mia is born. And with her birth comes days when Mia's father returns home from the auto shop, sits in a lawn chair outside the apartment, watches the sky blister in sunset, and his mind lifts, smile opening his grease-streaked face. He begins to believe he can support his family. Days he wakes and the apartment smells of his new baby. Cool milk. Honeyed. He listens to Mia breathe, the near inaudible inhales and exhales, the working of her lungs. That machine in parts running to keep his daughter alive, coddled in a perfect white sheet.

Moments Mia's parents understand the realness of their baby. Bathing her in the sink. Changing her diaper for the first time. Humming to her in the dark. Tracing her small lips with a finger. They brush her hair the length of her warm skull. They watch Mia's body transform—limbs inching longer, face molding to shape her personality, a shy smile. They see Mia take a first step. They marvel at her joy with which she stumbles alongside the couch. Joy—joy enchanting each nerve. There are minutes when her parents imagine a whole life. Before they sleep in bed together, feeling alone with their aches, betrayed by the night's brevity. Before neither can stand to be touched. Moments before the decrease in will, decrease of energy, missing work, increase in bruises, increase in distance between wanting to be better and trying, finding themselves lost sequentially in the years of their daughter's life.

One day Mia is suddenly six years old, and her father disappears into the desert. Later, Mia's mother looks in the mirror to find that no one is there. She thinks, *what if I left*. And a sense of peace spreads up her throat. She could sing. She screams. So this time she walks out the door, closes it firmly. Her shoes scuff hard dirt and the sky welcomes her. It's like swimming in the dead of summer. It's like falling asleep on a Friday night. She walks to the edge of a quiet road to travel west with strangers. Other people replace the people she's leaving. One morning, she's at the Pacific. There is no dimension. The blues have inhaled all sound. Sea birds sweep across her eyes.

When she stops walking, she sits in the courtyard of a homeless shelter in Los Angeles, beneath a thick fig tree. Some days the memory of water lifts her. She erases and re-etches needle marks.

One two three, ascendant.

Mia is six the last time she sees her father.

He's been missing for two weeks. She's still living with her mother at the time. One afternoon walking home from school she stops at an abandoned house as she does often, seeing the forgotten spaces as playthings. On the eastern part of the south shore, abandoned homes sit in a five-mile cluster surrounded by aloe and yucca, built for families who had sought employment at the resorts before they failed.

She chooses a house for the mint green color and date palm in the front yard which smells like warm sugar. The home hasn't been trashed yet, appearing still inhabited, save for the open, gaping drawers, unplugged appliances, naked mattresses. Human stains abundant.

Mia enters the kitchen through a sliding glass door. Standing on a chair, she rummages through cupboards, finds a stray plate, some utensils, and a bowl. She sets a place at the table, and sitting down, welcomes her family home for dinner.

Please pass the spaghetti, my love.

Her husband passes her the bowl.

Thank you, sweetie.

Her daughter hurries in from her bedroom.

How was school, Sandra?

Sandra is in a mood.

Her husband is tall with brown eyes. Her daughter looks just like Mia, long brown hair, soft-shaped face. Sun blinks across the floor, and Mia speaks to herself and into the afternoon. The hour elongates, deepens. She lingers in the stretch until a creak catches her ear, and breathing cuts, imaginary family vanishing from their seats at the dinner table. Someone's feet slide from inside the house, and her jaw sets tight, still.

Presence weighs behind the kitchen door. Shivers break from her small collarbone. The door opens to her father, bare-chested. His forearms are bruised. Blue eyes ring like fluorescent bulbs.

She hears her pulse in her ears, and he stares blankly at her, lips wilted until a smile rips across his face. He laughs—a hoarse pitch.

Voice comes from afar like tires crawling up gravel: What a trip. The Angel of Death brought me right here.

Mia can't move. Thoughts trip in a language of nerves. A breeze floats through the window carrying the bloody scent of mud. Mia scrunches her nose as she always does when smelling the Salton Sea. Her father sits at the table, groans, then bursts into laughter again. Stomach fat vibrating, rounding from a skeletal frame.

What in the hell, he says, spitting into the sunlight, sour breath mixing with the room's emptiness.

Pictures of a family they don't know hanging on the walls around them. Dusty Christmas garland trimming the sliding glass door. Her father leans back in his chair and looks at Mia with a smile.

What we eating?

Mia stares at his long fingernails, thick and chipping, permanent black grease lining his cuticles. His beard holds a blade of dead grass.

Why you look scared?

She shakes her head.

Use your words, Mia. No sense making talking hard. I've missed you, did you know?

I made spaghetti, she whispers.

You were talking to some people. I heard you.

He pulls the bowl to his chin and grabs one of the forks.

I wasn't talking to no one.

Did I ever tell you I had imaginary friends when I was little? My mom told me I threw 'em in the sea.

You throwed your friends in the sea? Mia's voice leaks. She folds into herself.

Don't remember really. Must of watched 'em drown. Got tired of them bossing me around.

Mia tucks her chin to her chest. Though it has only been two weeks since she last saw him, she doesn't remember her father looking so ill: his eyes glazed, moving like yellow Jell-O in their sockets, small red veins lighting up his cheeks. Discolored body.

Scary old dad wrecks everything, he says, taking a bite of invisible spaghetti, pursing his lips and pretending to slurp.

At six, Mia does not yet grasp how bodies can decay, how they are organisms which, when sick, wither like growing things from the earth.

I'm just staying here a little bit. I'll be back home soon I think. Do you ever just have to get away? Like going on a trip? He sets the bowl down and wipes the corners of his mouth with his wrists. That sure was good spaghetti, Mia.

I never went on a trip, she says.

You never 'gone' on no trip. Say you never 'gone'. Good English is important.

He cracks his knuckles.

Oh.

What kinda dad am I? If you could go anywhere, Mia, where would it be? I'm serious, go on, where would it be?

Mia thinks for a moment, eyes darting across the orange linoleum.

In class that week, Mia had been introduced to the solar system. Each planet described by its color and one or two facts, such as the rings of Saturn are made of ice, that a year on earth is 365 days, but that on Mercury a year is 88 days long. Jupiter has three moons, two more than earth.

Mia had enjoyed the art project portion, where students took Styrofoam balls and chose their favorite planet to replicate. Paint, glitter, sequins, pom-poms, pipe-cleaners, metallic beads. Mia chose Uranus, and when her father asks her where she wants to go, the image of the pure blue planet appears in her mind. Turquoise glitter. Strips of midnight blue construction paper she had pasted haphazardly across the cobalt paint. She closes her eyes. Her planet floats. The quiet distance fills her. Planets cradled by winds and tides of gravity.

Her teacher, Mrs. O'Neil, had said there are millions of miles between planets and stars. Millions. Do you know how much a million is, class?

Mrs. O'Neil emptied a box of 100 rubber bands.

Now, you would need 10,000 of these boxes to have a million rubber bands. Isn't that a lot? Earth is 150 million miles from the sun. Can you imagine all of the rubber bands? Can you just imagine?

Ur—ur-an-us, Mia whispers.

The hell did you just say?

Ur-an-us. I learnt about it in school. We learnt about space at my school.

Uranus? Why do you want to go there? You know it's the ass of the solar system.

Mia's voice rises from soft to eager: It's really blue and made out of clouds. Did you know that? There is lakes on Ur-an-us made out of diamond, like the pretty earrings. My teacher told me.

That so? A man could be rich on Uranus. But if it's made of clouds, how the hell are lakes on it?

Mia shrugs. It's space, she says.

I guess that's right.

He scratches his scalp, picks at the dead skin under his nails.

God got all sorts of weird shit up there, don't he? He says.

Her father's eyes suddenly darken, and his forehead gathers as if he's lost. He hugs himself, runs his own hands over his tattooed arms. A Celtic cross, ornate lines, fading green. A stick-and-poke four leaf clover. John 13:7.

Jesus replied, You do not realize now what I am doing, but later you will understand.

His stomach grumbles, and he covers his eyes with his palm, breathes through his nose.

God damn it, he says, shaking his head. God damn, I'm hungry.

He stands and his chair shoots back and hits the wall, causing a framed photo to fall.

Mia stands and walks to the picture, kneeling to see a family posing at the ocean. It isn't the Salton Sea, but the real ocean, the one Mia has never seen. The family has their arms wrapped around each other in a chain. The mother is laughing with her head thrown back, the two girls wearing swimsuits, and the dad has his hand on his waist, arm bent. Mia likes the way they all seem to be happy. She tries hanging the picture back on the wall, but she's too short. Her father takes the frame, and as he hangs it the coarse hair of his stomach grazes her forehead. He looks at the picture, then down at Mia. His cheeks carved, sternum severe.

What do you say we go on a trip? Just you and me. I'll have you home before your mom even notices. Let's us get some real dinner, okay?

He kneels to her level. He looks her straight in the eye, sweat highlighting his alien appearance. Face burned almost violet. Before that moment she can't remember seeing someone look so unlike themselves, so changed.

Mia doesn't want to go with him on a trip, but doesn't think she has a choice. When her father asks her to do something, she knows to do it. *Go to your room, Mia. Go out to play, Mia. Bring me a beer. Pray. Get on your knees and pray. Be a good girl.*

His face hovers before hers, lips rippling. Stray sentences fly from her mind, and she is left with nothing. She sees her father in the bright light of day, inexplicable and sick.

Ya know—you kinda' look like me, Mia, he says. Your face shape—the way your cheeks look all round.

His voice breaks off, and he stares in silence at her for a long time. She thinks about a very old person. Someone born so long ago that she can't imagine what their childhood would have been like. She thinks of death. And when a person dies, they go away on a very long trip. They are someone you can't talk to. Mia knows death is a sad thing. When someone is no longer a part of your life, you are supposed to cry.

Her father trembles.

He smells like the dead parts of the sea, where skeletons of cranes and mourning doves gather, where sun poaches mud and vapor.

I missed you, he says.

He smells like parts where the earth doesn't seem like the earth at all.

She's tasted salt water, but never the Pacific's salt, which is denser, and tastes like the amber plastics of kelp; salt which tastes subterranean, older than the world. Mia hasn't stood before the ocean, briny and magnetic, dismantling the body's rhythm.

The desert basin is expansive, but the space does not remember something primal. No elemental mists, as if each beach were an edge of the cosmos. Her mind can only recreate what she's seen on TV and in magazines.

Mia has never seen snow, never heard ice. She's never seen pines lighted by the moon. Never formed a snowball with her hands. She's never seen how slow snow can fall. Never seen an airplane close up, or a skyscraper. Never seen a jungle or a large city. She's never stood in a sea of people.

Because of Daniel's comment about her teeth, Mia doesn't smile in class. When she feels this upset, she lists: snow, an airplane, sea anemones, a humpback whale, the pyramids in Egypt, German castles, a tiger in India, the Great Wall of China, yellow cabs in New York, a tornado, a painter, tulips.

She likes to list the things she wants to see and places she wants to go. When she lists she doesn't think about the impossibility of any one thing, but the voice inside of her rises in pitch as she lists with more momentum, and she's going somewhere.

Sebastian sits across the classroom. His eyelids droop, mouth agape, large front teeth bleached with calcium deficiencies. Ms. Villa sits on a stool at the front of the classroom explaining the rules for their end-of-fifth-grade party. With a wave of her hand, students rush the large pizza boxes. Mia stays in her seat to watch Sebastian move into the crowd. She hopes that he'll glance her way, offer to grab her a slice. From her vantage, the sun crosses his irises, but he does not look at her. He leans into the others.

She continues the list, now pictures in her mind a feeling: *white foam. Blue glass, building of sky. Golden stone multiplied, pointing triangular toward the sun.*

Lucy sits down to tell Mia that Gabe, Lucy's boyfriend, has made out with a sixth grader.

No way, Mia says.

Lucy looks at the floor as she chips polish from her nails. Ms. Villa puts on *The Lion King*.

Aren't you going to eat? Lucy asks.

I'm not hungry, Mia says, then adds, Gabe is a slut.

Her voice lands heavily, awkward.

I think only girls can be sluts.

Oh.

Mia pauses, wanting to say more. Lucy's face holds an expression of confusion—she knits her brows and bites her bottom lip. Mia searches for the words to aid a friend scared of their own vulnerability, but she does not understand that such is the root of Lucy's expression. Mia can't yet make sense of the desire to see Lucy feel strong. She only understands that she wants Lucy to not feel sad.

You sure he kissed her? Mia asks.

Lucy nods.

That's really mean, Mia says.

It's all she can think to say, and Lucy touches her own neck, sighing. Ants crawl across the desk. A water leak near the sink has stained parts of the cream wall brown. The room smells like a crayon box, hot asphalt, and pepperoni. The air conditioner hums sadly. Mia wipes sweat from her forehead.

Orange stripes, yellow eyes. The ocean orange at dusk. The ocean a giant tide pool. Sand made of teeth. Deep water.

Why can't boys be sluts?

Lucy only shrugs. Mia says the word again. She whispers it, the *sss* a breeze between her teeth. With the *l* her tongue curls, the *t* touches the roof of her mouth, tongue drops to float.

The list trails off and her mother appears in her mind. She is walking toward Mia lined in gold, sun setting behind. Mia is four and there is a dead snake in the road, a tire mark indenting its concentrated body.

Mia is standing before the snake. Something churns behind like water rushing, or the sound of skinning your knee on gravel. Mia turns her head. A truck, a big rig. The engine a dark sound on a day just after rain when the breeze smells like coins. Mia's mother is wearing shorts, a glimpse of butt cheek through frayed denim, hips swinging wide as she runs toward Mia.

Come, come here, her mother shouts, hand outstretched. The engine's sound closer. Her mother screams.

The truck's breaks screech, a sound which scrapes the lingering scent of rain from the air. Before her mother jerks her away, Mia sees the snake's skin. The color of clouds. And then, she was on the sidewalk, face pressed against her mother's thighs, her mother's hand rubbing circles between Mia's shoulder blades. The truck driver leaning his head out the window, shouting, Is that your kid?

Mia and her mother walking away from him.

Control your kid, lady, and put on some god-damn clothes. Slut.

Mia remembers that her mother had been angry with the man, had slapped Mia across her face for running into the street. Her mother had begun to cry, and maybe she had felt sad and angry with the man the way Mia feels angry at Gabe now.

It's not fair, she thinks. He isn't being fair.

Lucy walks toward the pizza. Her shoulders watch the room.

Mia watches her friend, then looks at Sebastian. He's talking to Daniel and Benny, hands moving to emphasize his words.

Sometimes at night, she falls asleep facing his back and her legs slide close behind his. Sometimes she can't sleep, but looks at the sky and feels his back breathing into her stomach. She wonders how darkness and breathing, the rhythm she feels and doesn't see, can make her feel safe. Mia remembers the hundreds of things she can feel at any moment, and how those things disappear when she is touching him.

Sebastian a castle. Sebastian the Pacific. Sebastian a field of tulips. Sebastian eating ice cream. Chocolate on his lips, hands near her. He rubs circles on her back.

She makes herself beautiful, over and over and over.

When the 2:50 bell rings, fifth grade ends. On the playground, Lucy wipes her tears as she hugs Mia. Before Lucy walks away, Mia says, Maybe he didn't mean it. Who knows, maybe it didn't happen.

Mia sits at a picnic table waiting for Sebastian and his friends. She's going to watch the boys skate, as she does some days after school. Across the playground Sebastian, Daniel, and Benny throw pebbles at each other, kick at each other's shins. Sebastian is the slower of the three, and Mia watches him lumber about. Only last year he had been shorter than Mia. Now, he stands a half-foot taller. Mia sits as straight as she can, feels beads of sweat slip between her breasts and down her stomach.

Steely sky. A hawk echoes. She looks toward the mountains in the background, thick-muscled, earth russet, and thirsty. No clouds alleviate or provide the expanse dimension. Space vacuums back without grip. The advent of summer makes the silence of the day more noticeable.

The boys and Sebastian approach her. Fluid movement jerked by occasional bouts of laughter and joggling arm gestures toward one another, energy piqued in their heels when they speak. Daniel's head is tilted back, exposing his neck as if he means it to stick out farther than his face. His large eyes dart about, but attract back to her every few seconds.

She squints into the sun, feeling the urge to swallow, but forgetting how to when she thinks about the muscles in her throat. She wishes she could blend into the light the way darkness erases a person. In the dark, there is breathing and touching and smelling, but nothing to see.

Mia knows that Daniel's leg was bitten by a German Shepard six months ago, and she knows his oldest brother shot himself in the family's shed. She knows he was the kid in their class accusing other kids of having wet dreams, and he called Ms. Villa a skinny whore with just-okay-tits. Mia knows these things about Daniel because this is a small class in a small school in a small town. Daniel and the other students know that she doesn't have parents. She wonders if Daniel looks at her breasts, if he calls them *tits*, if he talks about their size, and she sits even straighter, abs pinned to her spine. The boys circle around.

Better make sure scar-face gets home, Sebastian. Daniel flicks Mia on the shoulder and she slaps at his hand.

You're a douche bag, she says.

You don't even know what that means, do you? Daniel says.

Mia looks at Sebastian. Their eyes meet, but then he looks to the asphalt.

I do, she says.

Tell me when you figure out how to clean your dirty pussy, Daniel says.

Mia has heard the word *pussy* before, but she's not entirely sure what it means. She knows the word belongs to a woman. It's something a woman has.

Her mind searches for grounding, but thought speed escalates— mind a blurred screen. And while she'd felt the day's temperature prior to that moment, suddenly she feels sick the way a fever aches in the joints, spins the head with a thread twisted in her stomach. She wants a wind to pick her up and rip her away. She doesn't want to walk, or run, or even fly, but to be ripped from the picture.

Your brother's dead, she says.

Daniel stops laughing and grabs her, squeezes her forearm muscle, stares at her like she is a dying animal. She can feel her bone pinched.

Shut up, bitch—homeless bitch, he says, shoving her.

Sebastian reaches toward her, but Mia dips her shoulder.

Don't touch me, she says.

Her naked body appears in her mind, and shame rivets her frame. She flips through her parts, each image burning more than the previous.

Cheek, neck, back, throat.

That morning, Mia's anger had fueled the way her legs took stride, the pendulum swing of her hips. But now, as she begins to walk away, her body feels awkward, almost absurd: the tight grate and burn of one thigh against another, her chest jutting from her body.

Thighs, hips, breasts.

With each step she feels the new excess of her figure quiver. These parts of her feel wrong—too sensitive and too soft. These parts feel as obtrusive and ugly as the cigarette burns on her face, the brown marks on her teeth.

Sebastian runs up from behind, places his hand on her shoulder, thumb pressing her collarbone. The pressure running from thumb placement to deeper in, to the muscle beneath muscle. An urgency she senses in the depth, as if his grabbing onto her is a way of speaking. Words with meat. He is a voice in the dark.

Bone, breath, shoulders, hands, sleep. Fuck you.

Fuck off, Mia says, and like *slut*, the words feel heavy. She doesn't like to speak to Sebastian that way, using harsh language. She'd heard Val say it to the news on television. And her father, long ago, telling her mother to fuck off. Or Fuck this place. Fuck everything. And she'd heard Sebastian say Fuck, God damn fuck, fuck, fuck, when he cut into his pinky slicing a fat watermelon. The blood absorbed into the blushing fruit.

Mia, listen, they're just messing with you. Don't take it so seriously, Sebastian says. Thumb against her bone, harder.

The pressure is a word. The muscle beneath muscle is a word. She doesn't know how to say it, how to say those boys make her feel *ugly*. She doesn't know how to say that the boys make her feel worthless.

Sebastian sees Mia's eyes lighten with tears, brown iris honeyed. Daniel shouts from down the playground, Come on, man, let her go if she wanna go. But Sebastian doesn't, though his thumb eases against her, the pressing no longer asking for more.

Mia appears smaller than he remembers. Not in terms of body size or height, but in his sense of her. She appears as a light, and maybe this is the first time in Sebastian's life that he sees Mia's soft gaze, and her hair glows around her face. With his arm remaining on her shoulder, he steps back from her, from this new warmth he has discovered, if only through sympathy.

Come on, Benny shouts.

Mia and Sebastian hear Daniel spit. The breeze is a thick rope. Mia sees Sebastian's expression release tension. To Mia, his eyes say: we're okay. You and me, Sebastian and Mia—we are okay.

Mia, just come, Sebastian says. Come with us.

She can't bring herself to turn from him, to detach his hold. And she doesn't want to walk off by herself. She wants to watch Sebastian skate, watch his body bounce, teeter into the air, muscles catch, and glide into balance. Mia shifts her weight, sighs. She doesn't want to be alone, doesn't want to walk into an empty house only to wait for Sebastian to return later. He's touching her, linking her to him.

Fine, she says.

Together they walk toward Daniel and Benny. Sebastian's shoes scrape the gravel. Mia's pink dress is a soft cloud in his peripheral and Sebastian is everything in Mia's—the peach color of his cheeks, the heavy swing of his arms.

All done crying, Mia? Daniel says, his whole chest puffed. He's wearing jersey shorts. The dog bite left a deep scar on his calf, flesh still crimson and puckered. Sebastian had seen Daniel be bitten by the German Shepard. Flesh ripping open, muscle metallic, veins threading the shine. Sebastian's throat tightening, bizarre and screaming. Sebastian told Mia the blood could have filled their bathtub. It was like seeing someone shot, Sebastian said, though he'd never seen someone shot. For all of the dead discovered along the Salton Sea, neither of them had seen a dead body. Daniel had pleaded, *Let me go, please, stop. Please, stop,* his voice emerging from a buried place.

Daniel's limp is hard, not weak, as if hurling himself forward. When someone asks about his leg, he details the attack like a war story, gaining adrenaline as he recounts the crunch of his own bone. Same sound as chewing glass, he'd say. He can't skate normally yet, but he rides gently around the pool in which his friends skate, criticizing form or congratulating a good heelflip or noseblunt.

Don't cry, Mia. We'll be nicer. Promise. Benny's voice is disingenuous, split by laughter.

Mia rolls her shoulders back and smiles directly at them both. Daniel shakes his head and turns, dropping his skateboard. In a single motion he steps onto the board and pushes off with delicate caution. Benny sails onto his own board and races beyond the playground's chain link fence.

I want to keep up with them, Sebastian says.

Mia jogs alongside Sebastian as he glides on his board. She feels lighter.

They leave the school yard, bleed into Marina Sal. A town perpetually empty. Cracked, cracking, fumes in the air, dehydrated fragments of retro blue and steel, gas and sun. The town is a set, and all of the lights are turned on, switches and back-drops exposed. No one wants to remember the story it told. They pass a deserted auto shop, shelled and dark copper, sunken. On one of the cement walls, graffiti:

SPACES NEAR TO ME,
BEAUTY I CANNOT FATHOM,
AND YOU'RE STUCK IN TIME.

A pounding heart and all else is silence. Desert sparrows run arabesques above them. The birds, little brown arrows. Quiet is the crinkling asphalt and weeds. Mia's skin amasses sunlight. Her breath hot. Her heart flies.

Mia and Sebastian have jogged nearly a mile from the schoolyard. Daniel and Benny are several hundred feet in front of them. Sebastian squints toward the Blue Palm Hotel, a smoke-colored Spanish influence building abandoned three decades ago. Mia jogs with one hand holding down her skirt. The day's air is dense, hugging her each step.

Benny disappears into the Blue Palm through an opening in a boarded window. Daniel follows, lifting and inserting his wounded leg carefully through the narrow opening. Mia and Sebastian approach the hole, faces illumed, plump with oxygen. Mia's lungs pulling from deep in her torso.

Go ahead, Sebastian says, pointing to the window.

Her chest expands widely to slow her heart. She grips a board across the window, ducks, and glides into the hotel's nebulous cavern.

Mia remembers being inside many abandoned buildings throughout her childhood, but none are as gaping as the Blue Palm. She is familiar with the space. Tarps line the room's circumference— squatter's beds. In the dimness Mia can see mounds throughout the foyer, piles of possessions. Green pieces of plastic stretch across diamond shapes patterned into the domed ceiling, plastic applied by people sleeping in the space, desiring only the subtlety of light. Darkness is emerald in air and tar-like in shadow, and barely-there dust motes grow from the diamonds. Mold emits patches of cooler temperature throughout the room. Gaps between coolness are sour and warm with body odor, or hard from sand tracked in, or charred from extinguished fire pits once fueled by alcohol and trash.

Mia wades the darkness, passing piles of things, empty liquor bottles, grease-stained paper bags, a baseball bat chewed at the handle, pillows, knotted shirts, dirty shoes. The sleeping bags are giant black centipedes. Contained in their individual spaces, the piles appear like tumors inside the body's own darkness.

Laughter whips through the room, through her: Daniel's voice echoes, and she cannot see him, but thinks he's down a hall straight ahead. She hears Sebastian's steps approach her from behind, and then he breathes near her and she listens.

Gravity is suddenly wispier, dreamy—her body is hers and also something floating with ease in indistinct lighting. Each bone shifting into weightlessness. Her density pieced apart, she only an idea of herself. She watches herself from afar.

But Sebastian stands behind her thinking that he can't see Daniel and Benny. He plugs his nose, breathing through his mouth. Squinting, he searches for movement in the vague recesses. Sebastian isn't thinking about Mia's form close to his.

Where did they go? Mia says.

She peers over her shoulder. Sebastian a silhouette—green outlines him. Her voice is fragile, and she lifts one hand to touch Sebastian's face before he answers, her tongue shaping to say his name. She is veiled; he is backlit. *Sebastian,* she wants to say, *here I am. I'm here.* But this exchange doesn't occur.

Get the little bitch over here, Daniel says.

Daniel is a voice tight between Mia's shoulder blades. A stitch.

She remembers there was a night years ago—Mia and Sebastian were nine years old—when a faceless man knocked on the door of their home. The two had been watching *The Jungle Book* on VHS and eating tater tots in the living room. Mia had just woken from a nap. She hadn't napped during the day in a long time, but had fallen asleep exhausted after she and Sebastian had pretended to be Olympic athletes, running races up and down their street for hours. Sun-induced sleep. Leaden limbs. Purple sky.

When she awoke, she was certain days had passed. Light no longer fanned across her legs. Her mouth was tight like she hadn't spoken a word in weeks. Her lips and legs itched. Sweat glued her shirt to her body, and she'd dreamt that tiny spiders had emerged from the creases in her palms. She inhaled and the evening rushed in and her body did not have a description for the sensation of time lapse. She heard music, and so wandered from Sebastian's bedroom to find *The Jungle Book*, drawings verdant and fuzzy, radiant on the TV screen. She sat beside Sebastian and he smiled at her. His socks too big for his feet. He was missing both incisors.

The knock sounded, Val rose from the kitchen table and answered. Mia and Sebastian heard the door close, could just make out Val's voice on the front step until it faded into the movie's sound. Many minutes passed. The tater tots warm in Mia's slow-moving mouth. Tension weighed above her eyebrows, a slight pound within her head. Who had been at the door? She was discombobulated, concerned that she had lost something, hours or sunlight. Her stupor looped. The movie was and wasn't playing, moving forward. She rubbed her tender eyes. Val had been gone for a long time.

Mia had stood and walked to the window, pressed her cheek against the cool glass, able to glimpse the front step. Val and the visitor were not there. Mia walked back to her place beside Sebastian, and the tension in her head grew into a beat—beat, beat, beat—perfect rhythm. She could no longer bring herself to chew the food. Closed her eyes, but the muscles in her legs wanted to move, walk through the house. The sliding glass door in the kitchen opened just as Mia passed. The stars had shown up. Yellow stove light splashed Mia, and painted Val's red eyes wet.

Val?

Come with me, Mia.

The two had lain on Val's bed, and she'd held Mia.

Why are you crying, Val?

Will you fall asleep with me tonight? Val's voice close to Mia's ear.

In Val's room, all lights were off, and a black-out sheet stretched across the window. Mia watched digital numbers on the alarm clock count up. She wanted a glass of water, but didn't want to disturb Val. Because she had slept through the afternoon, Mia couldn't fall asleep.

Val's breath moved like the blood moving through Mia's body. Sebastian came, slept on the other side of Val.

Water the color of the trees in the *Jungle Book*, vivid and cool. Mia swallowed, and it was 5 AM. It was the first long night of Mia's life. A long night following a day erased.

The next morning Mia had asked Sebastian if he knew why Val had been crying.

It was my dad, Sebastian had said. He didn't look at her.

And seconds are doing it again in the Blue Palm—seconds are viscous, slow churned—she feels more and more herself in relation to the moment. She's watching clock numbers pass as if the next minute will never come.

Mia repeats his voice in her head: *Get the little bitch over here.*

Sebastian's hand is now on her shoulder, and she hopes he will pull her back and against him. He will pull her back through the gap in the window, into the last day of fifth grade, back onto the empty streets, and maybe they will get ice cream, maybe they will return home and spray their feet and legs with the hose, maybe they will lie beneath the swamp cooler, cold air flowing through their hair and over their necks, laughing chests, and maybe Sebastian will slice her a mango, sticky, succulent, and they will spend a long afternoon together at the face of longer days, a summer, sun-dominated, with short, watercolor nights.

But those moments are not this moment. Sebastian's hand makes a pressure that pushes Mia forward, not back. She doesn't move, and so he presses his hand against her left shoulder blade.

Mia?

He leans, and she steps forward. They walk toward the hallway, a long corridor lined by identical rooms. Mia can see that all of the doors are closed, maybe concealing sleepers, the sun-sick, shadows, maybe a woman and a small child.

Her heart is big like the dark. Implausible like the place. She's scared. Though she feels invisible in the sunless room, the boys seem to see her more clearly.

She shivers—skin feels electric.

Touch her and she'd shock you. Touch her and she'd cry.

Mia is seven.

From the mountains coldness drips into autumn's heat. The conflicting airs engender silver, a spare fog which stretches over the Salton Sea, erasing the horizon. It's a Sunday morning. Sun a satin circle. Mia and her mother are being kicked out of their apartment on Thanksgiving day.

Mia's father hasn't been offering financial support for over a year, and her mother has been struggling to keep consistent waitressing hours. Val offers her couch to them for a few weeks, and Mia and her mother are transitioning the few things they own to Val's garage.

Most possessions Mia's mother has managed to sell: the couch for twenty dollars, pots and pans fifty cents each. For the television, she managed thirty-five dollars. The VCR went for ten. A weight set, five to fifteen pounds, which Mia's mother had purchased years ago, hoping then to lose weight, sold for three dollars. She doesn't have any fat left on her body. Months of speed and her bones have pushed out into ravines. Her spine a thick chain. She doesn't want any more stuff. Everything, she doesn't want it.

The drug use began months before the move, when Mia's mother met a man who had claimed to have seen God's hand.

Palm. Pinky. Pointer. Middle. Ring finger. Thumb.

From Las Vegas, he'd caught a ride to Marina Sal with a truck driver packing cattle for a slaughter house near El Centro. The man's name was Moscow. Mia's mother sat next to him on a wooden barstool. The hand had reminded Moscow of his father's hands—calloused and hard, when his father had reached middle age, a stretch when both childhood and old age are impossible to understand.

God wrote 'numbered, numbered' on my bedroom wall. Just his hand showed, nothing else. His hand came out of thin air, I swear to it. And God used a Sharpie.

What does that mean? she asked. What's numbered?

My days, Moscow said. My days are numbered. God showed himself to me five years ago. I left Kansas and never have I looked back at it. I know if I do, bad shit will happen. You don't test the words that show special just for you.

They were sitting in a Brawley bar, hole-in-the-wall, metallic smoke. Mia's mother had been drinking since the afternoon. Bubbles popping against her brain.

She was skipping her shift at Imperial Chinese Restaurant, because she couldn't stand to look one more moment at the faded paper lanterns hanging over each table. Didn't want to smell frozen fish thawing in front of a space heater. Didn't want to serve the regulars, most of them elderly men, who had nothing better to do on weekdays but go out for lunch alone and chew their food with open mouths, orange chicken smeared on their jowls. The manager, Michael, was an elementary school friend who never had the heart to fire her for missing shifts. He grew up with a single mother, and he remembered the mornings his mother brought stolen bread home for breakfast. The nights she wouldn't eat at all so that his brothers and sisters could. When Michael would pass Mia's mother in the restaurant's backroom, or slide past her in the kitchen as she was gathering trays to serve, he could smell, faintly, her sweat, traces of soap, a floral shampoo mixed with pot sticker steam. When he could smell her body, he missed his mother, the way after a long day she too still smelled beautiful, and exhausted—a personal, exposing scent.

She'd taken the bus straight to Brawley, hadn't even bothered to call to say that she was sick. Fall in the Sonoran Desert reminded her of her father. He'd return home from work with dark purple heads of broccoli and soft pears, and she missed those cool evenings with him, the silk fabric of memory: something luxurious and easy about the earth, raw produce, raw color, early sunset. The afternoon paused and the autumn effervesced. Her father's calloused hands not unlike God's. Brilliant resins glowing beneath his fingernails.

She didn't know that she trembled, or that she was a silhouette in a dirty bar, or that she sat more in the past playing out dreams. Outside, the sun burnt surfaces. People were waiting for her.

She hadn't seen her husband in months. She slouched closer to Moscow.

What are you doing with your numbered days? She asked.

Wasting nothing. Looking straight 'head. I've got it figured I'll see one more miracle, then poof, I'll turn to smoke and on up to heaven I go.

I hope I see heaven. Sometimes I don't think it's real.

Don't say that. Jesus can hear you. He can hear your every thought.

Jesus got bored with me, I'm sure of it. I don't know much, anyhow.

He slid his hand over her thigh. She was padded, soft plastic. But his hand was hot, that much she could sense. The hotness dipping into her. She dipped her head toward his chest. He smelled like the desert at night.

She said, I used to be good with numbers. I could multiply anything in my head. Jesus could tell you how many stars there are and were ever and will ever be in his head.

She imagined a camera racing through space and this camera was actually God and seeing was believing and she was believing in God and the universe and how nothing, not a single thing, could last long enough to feel like it really happened, even each autumn. Lebbeck trees dusting the earth white. Her father's arthritic hips, how his steps took a square shape.

Moscow hugged her close to his chest, and she spent the next two weeks with him, holed up in an abandoned house. The drug started with goose bumps through her arms, and then her heart seemed to swallow air, big gulps of air, and the heart became a thing in itself, moved about the chest with a mind of its own, spurring jolts to begin—blood feathered through her hands, euphoria tickling all the thoughts she had beneath her skin; her pulse a fountain. She couldn't stop talking. Couldn't stop thinking.

Then she was staring through a sunset. I'm not ready to die yet, she said to no one in particular. Drifters, strangers surrounding her. I'm not ready to die yet. She couldn't stand still. She tapped one foot and then the next.

Her mouth raced: My eyes feel like they are astronauts.

I could have been a banker.

I want to ride the New York subway.

I want to be in a crowd of people and I want a man to walk up to me and I want him to hand me his business card and I want him to say, *Will you be a model?*

I want to be taller.

Love more, love more.

I'm not ready to die yet.

For once, go all the way.

She slept beside a fire, dangerously close. Flames pasted on her softest dipping flesh: too thin, cooking. Fire smelled, surely, like time. Stoves, campfires, fireplaces, sunburn, morning breath, dead brush. Her jaw felt as if she'd been crunching ice.

Where should she live? This is a question.

This is nauseating and cold.

Val had been searching for her, and eventually the large bonfire caught her eye. She had stayed off the drug for a few days, but it wasn't difficult to come by in Marina Sal. She missed the way she'd felt intelligent, a wide lens.

She had been in danger of losing the apartment long before she began using speed, but the addiction finalized debts. She never returned to work. She'd felt a weight lift from her shoulders when she received the seizure notice. The sheets, after all, no matter how often she'd washed them, still smelled like her husband. Sweat, to be in love with a person's body in release.

The living room had held the crib that Mia's father built. The living room with its brown carpet. Wallpaper mauve and palpable with lamp glow. The kitchen, grease and stale cigarettes, where they'd drank $1.50 bottles of Cabernet, played cards, held each other by the knees and elbows, gripping through each other.

She wanted to live in a place where nothing could transport her. Where she didn't feel the need to apologize to walls, linens, the texture of afternoon light.

That morning she takes the last box to the street with the other boxes. There are only four. Three contain Mia's clothes, her dolls, blankets, picture books. She has one box—some clothes, a casserole dish from her own mother, an album from her parents' wedding, her mother's lace veil, a stone her father had lifted from the earth while walking one evening, a stone he carried in his pocket for its smoothness. He'd turn it in his palms with his eyes closed.

She has her father's copy of *The Call of the Wild*, and a framed photo of her mother in front of the Modern Art Museum in Palm Springs. Her mother is wearing red lipstick. She also has a cigar tin inside the box. The tin holds a lock of baby Mia's hair, and each one of Mia's baby teeth. There is the bracelet she wore in the hospital when she gave birth. A polaroid of Val when Val is sixteen, sunny and over-exposed. Val's red corduroy shorts high, her legs long. She has her quiet smile. And there is also a picture of her and Val in the back seat of the car. She and Val nursing. The sun rising. Their breasts swollen.

She does not keep anything from Mia's father.

These things, all that she has. Parts of her parents. Parts lost from Mia. It all happened at some point, but can never be relived. She wishes that each item could belong to someone more deserving. Her eyes sting with tears that don't fall.

Mia walks outside, sees her mother staring at the four boxes.

Mommy, are we all done?

She smiles, nodding. When she nods, her skin stretches over muscle in her neck. When her mother hugs her, Mia feels like she's hugging the trunk of a palm tree. Mia doesn't like to see her mother so thin. Months before, her mother had been soft, legs and breasts rounder, inviting to lean into.

Mia begins to walk down the cement steps.

Wait, her mother says. Don't you want to say goodbye?

Goodbye?

To home. Let's say goodbye to home.

Mia looks over her shoulder. She's left the front door ajar and can glimpse the living room. She hadn't thought about the actual parting with the apartment until that moment.

Yes, Mia says.

Let me finish this, her mother says, lighting a cigarette and turning back to her memories.

Mia walks back through the front door. The living room is warm—encapsulated sunlight, hours old. How naked the space appears, void of furniture. The ceiling seems taller to Mia. The corners breathe. She eyes indentions in the carpet where a chest of drawers, couch, and cabinet had sat for years. Mia suddenly wants to smooth away the indentions. The past presenting itself to her. Imprints making her long for a moment in time when her father still appeared every morning, and breakfast sizzling, the scent of food absorbing into the fabric of her pajamas.

Mia sits in the center of the empty room. Minutes later her mother opens the screen door, pauses, and lets it slam behind her. She slides onto her stomach beside Mia.

Looks different, doesn't it? Her mother says.

Goodbye, house, Mia says.

Her mother muffles her voice with her hand, says, Goodbye, Mia.

They both laugh, and then their bodies sink into stillness, enjoying the day's warmth. Empty rooms quieter. Minutes blending, and the afternoon becomes a final minute. Her mother rolls onto her back, stretching her arms horizontally, chest bones rippling.

I have an idea, her mother says.

She stands and takes a pen from her purse, a Sharpie she'd used to label the few packed boxes. She beckons Mia to follow her to the bathroom. The two stand before the mirror over the sink.

Does mommy look different, Mia?

Different. Mia nods. Thin. Her mother appears weak, and Mia has never thought her mother as weak before.

I know.

Her mother looks at her own reflection for several minutes, turning her face left and right, eyeing angles of her pointed jaw.

Do you know what God is, sweetheart?

Yes, Mia thinks, she does know. God lives in the sky and he made the world. Her father had taught her how to pray. A year ago, the day before he left the family. The memory a tendril.

Praying will come in handy, and someone needs to teach her how, he said. They kneeled by her bed and he said bow your head and bring your hands together, palm to palm, and talk to God. When Mia asked how to talk to God, he said, you're talking to everything. To your bed, to the sky, to your own two hands. God made all of that. Her father said, Listen to me pray. Dear God, thank you for my daughter, Mia, and thank you for believing in me. Thank you for thinking I'm not a bad guy, and thank you for times like this when it's dark and cool and Mia and me are talking to you. Please bring us some peace in our dreams, and please keep us together forever.

Her mother's voice: Sweetheart, do you know what God is?

God lives on clouds and he made everything, Mia says.

Did you know God talked to me once?

Mia didn't know God could talk back to a person. She doesn't pray often, but when she does, he never answered her.

God wrote on a wall, her mother says. A hand appeared out of thin air, Mia, and God wrote the word 'Numbered, Numbered'.

Mia has goose bumps, looking at her mother. She imagines the blank wall, hand appearing in lingering sun and the words written in black ink.

Why did he say that? Mia asks.

Her mother is silent for a beat, thinking about the way Moscow had answered. Her days are numbered, too. She feels this is a certainty, a projection as definite as anticipating Christmas.

So still, her mother stands as if she isn't breathing.

Mommy?

Everything can be counted. Do you understand that, Mia? You can count anything with numbers, and you can add or take away and it matters how much you want or how little you need.

Mia isn't sure what her mother means, or why her mother begins to cry. She doesn't know how to ask her mother to clarify, or what kind of clarification she needs, and so Mia is silent, wanting to be held. She wants her mother to stop talking and to hold her.

You. Her mother points at Mia. Plus me. Her mother points back at herself. We're more together.

Her mother's cheeks heave back as she smiles, or winces. Mia tilts her head to the side, staring up at her mother, or at a part of her mother—her bones seem lonely, eyes empty.

Goodbye home, Mia thinks. Goodbye something else, too. Something much more difficult to put words to. Words make real of what Mia can't touch. Here, a feeling of fear. And if she can't say it and she can't touch it, that feeling, then what is it? She doesn't want to see her mother cry. The sight makes Mia's stomach coil. It makes her angry.

Her mother takes the cap off the pen, and writes on the bathroom mirror: M & M 1992.

Like the candies, Mia says.

Her mother stares at the mirror, hand hovering mid-air. Light crystal slats, dust iridescent. Her mother's hand hangs, pen resting between slender fingers. Her mother is disconnected, and she is disembodied, and she is holy in her smallness, ghostly in her translucence. And Mia has no words and no way to touch her mother's sadness.

All the things that could have been written, but where to begin. Why those words and why not others? Mia stands close to her mother's legs, but her mother wants to move away, pull away, the way muscles contract when cold, pulling and hardening toward the bone—her mother wants to pull away, harden, harden, and then break, turn to powder, to blue. To the autumns her daughter can count.

Her mother begins to hum.

| *ii* |

Mia and Sebastian walk down a hallway in the Blue Palm. Daniel and Benny are shadows at first in the darkness, hovering at the end of the corridor. As she walks, the walls appear to close-in the nearer she approaches the boys, before they disappear from sight. Mia passes through a doorway and into one of the hotel rooms; Daniel and Benny are there, now three-dimensional, textured. Depth of light from a boarded window carves their necks, chests. Mia can make out that Benny is crouched in a corner, and that Daniel stands, leaning against a wall. The room has trapped air, body odor pasted atop body odor; trapped air in the dark feels more like a paint color, less an element to be collected in the lungs.

She wonders what to say, and she wonders how to stand amongst the boys. She wonders what they want. Sebastian stands behind her and though he isn't touching her, his proximity offers a sense of comfort. She tells herself: nothing could be wrong if Sebastian is here. And this is just how Mia feels Sebastian's presence, that he is and has been the person breathing next to her in the middle of the night.

What's going on? Mia asks. She looks over her shoulder to find Sebastian's gaze, but he stares beyond her. His jaw is set rigid in a way she doesn't recognize.

Sebastian?

He's silent in response.

She places her hand over the center of her chest. Mute firecrackers, breathing. She tries to calm her body, to appear uninhibited. Why wouldn't Sebastian answer her? Sometimes when she and Sebastian are with his friends, he is not the same Sebastian— less attentive, less silly. She's grown used to the switch, and when they return home, he always transforms back into her best friend. Though this time, his presence feels different. Suddenly Sebastian seems much bigger behind her, as if he were a grown man.

Daniel is sharp in the dark, not a body, but a part of the architecture. And Benny, a part of the light, or lack of it. Sebastian doesn't seem to care. Mia thinks that maybe Daniel finally pushed the teasing too far. Sebastian is slow, too tall. Sebastian is sloppy when he eats, raised in a trash can. His face is dirty, and his head is over-sized. Sebastian is ugly. Daniel loves to say, "Sebastian, you're one ugly motherfucker."

Mia wonders if that Sebastian—the different one amongst his friends, does whatever he's told—is now the only Sebastian. But when did she lose the other? Did it happen just today? This afternoon? Was it something she did, or didn't do?

She doesn't want to lose him.

Mia steps back, wondering if Sebastian will move, but he does not. Her back falls, softly, into his chest.

She doesn't linger, steps to the side, and looks at him. His mouth twists to speak, but clamps, holding back. He shifts his weight, and the movement makes waves behind her.

She steps closer to Daniel, the colorless architecture. The scent of midnight and flesh unbathed, liquor steaming in pores, bad dreams—this room a container—Mia takes a deep breath to steady herself, and the scents bring a sense of dejection. She feels, beneath her fear, a pull to forgotten things.

/

To Sebastian, Mia appears taller in the dark. Her hair feathers, catching dim light from the boarded window. There is suddenly an aura about her, but he cannot see anything other than her silhouette. She might as well be any girl, or naked. A ghost. There is a part of him that wants to reach out and touch her.

Instead he touches a memory:

six years old and at the zoo in Palm Springs, celebrating his birthday with his mom. He'd always wanted to see giraffes, and it had been better than he expected—the spotted animals with dark, caring eyes, black licorice tongues, their hugeness blooming mythic. When the babies galloped, muscles quivered, legs fluid yet mechanical as if the animal was an invention from the future. Sebastian felt an immense pleasure seeing a living thing almost too beautiful to be real.

Mom, Mom! Look!

A small giraffe noticed a white butterfly. It extended its long neck toward the floating insect, head bobbing gently, and when the butterfly drifted away the giraffe jumped toward it, legs swinging its body into motion.

Mom, look! Sebastian jumped too.

After the giraffe, Sebastian saw a green-eyed leopard. Wolves. Parrots sherbet and glossy. Pepper-colored foxes, bodies twitching like they were whispering to him.

His mom held his hand as they browsed the reptiles. Ball python, bearded dragon, an iguana as huge as his own torso. When they approached a chameleon, Sebastian pressed his face hard against the glass. A rich fuchsia, its body nimble, feet and tail curved in thick ringlets, and tiny eyes revolving in its head like a robot's. And then suddenly the pink color became neon green.

Mom, did you see that?!

The revolving eye struck his movement, and Sebastian froze, enchanted. Green dyed yellow.

Was his mom seeing it too, the changes in colors, the pinball eyes? Mom? Why does that lizard change colors?

It's called a chameleon, Sebastian. They change colors 'cuz it's their way of hiding themselves. If he turns green and he's in a tree, the animals who want to eat him won't see him all that well.

Wow.

Don't you wish humans could do that?

Do what?

She stared at the changing animal.

Camouflage, Val said.

The memory rushes through Sebastian, and with it, he imagines his mom in the room too, as if she were there to disapprove of their presence in the dark. Though she is far from the Blue Palm, Sebastian feels Val staring at him, eyes glittering like cut glass. He shivers.

How many people were hiding in this abandoned building? The creaking of the sleeping bodies somewhere in other rooms, or the shifting apparition of inertia: scrape up off the floor, inch toward an opening, smell light.

Mia's silhouette—an underexposed tree. The image of her causes Sebastian to envision that she could, if she wished, change into any new and impossible thing, beyond his or Daniel's or Benny's expectations.

/

Aren't you going to skate? Mia asks.

Daniel slides into some light. He stands before her slatted by deep blue—the blue which is the blue of cracking things. Late hours or empty landscapes.

Mia, Daniel says, take off your dress.

The words don't shock her, but time, which has been slow—those digital numbers—collapses. She had known what he wanted, but how did she know? How many glimpses had she caught of a woman's naked body on the TV, Val watching some movie. Technicolor breathing when two people move into one another—panting making steam from the screen's glow. There were times when Mia could almost feel it, that breathing, the color of the scene filling their living room.

When Mia saw that kind of touching in a movie, she wanted to be alone with it. She wanted to sit close to the TV and watch and rewind and watch.

She felt beautiful when she watched those scenes, imagining herself as an adult woman, a wisp of a perfect, future self, tucked into

Sebastian's arms—his sense of self solidified by warmth and sweetness. He's holding her because he cares. He doesn't want anything bad to happen to her, this future Sebastian.

There was a night when Val went to bed and Mia pushed in a tape as Sebastian played a Gameboy on the floor, eyes glued to the tiny green screen. He didn't notice that she was fast-forwarding—the movie blurring by like a river. She paused when the two people moved to make love. Hands finding the waist or neck. Mouth meeting mouth. She watched the moment flicker, and turned to find Sebastian transfixed. As he watched, unblinking, she felt a sense of power. The sensation spread through her chest, up her throat, and she smiled.

That night, she felt as if she were the thing actually transfixing him.

Mia doesn't move.

She thinks about earlier that morning when she had dressed, her nakedness reflected back at her. In the privacy of that moment her body was somehow a relative of the light bouncing off the bodies of other naked women in her memory, the ones stretched out briefly, in clips, across the screen.

If Daniel wants her to take off her dress, he must like her, have love for her. Mia reasons: this is how it works on TV—the man has love for a woman, and he takes off her clothes and he touches her, holds her. Daniel's shoulder bends downward as his body sinks to the side, babying his wounded calf. His head tilting back, hands folding across his hips. But he has never acted in a loving way toward her. He has never been gentle toward her, not that she could remember. He had never said a nice thing to her.

Isn't that what you want? Take it off, Daniel says.

His scar is jagged, severe, and at the same time, tender like the roots of very old trees. An entire bathtub full of blood. A bathtub of blood like a bathtub of syrup. Daniel stands beside her, sweat hot upon his brow.

She places her palms on her sides. She feels the impressionable quality of herself; if she pushes long enough, she'll leave red marks or bruises or maybe even change her shape. Daniel's injured calf appears deflated. And suddenly Mia can imagine that Daniel is curious about how Mia's body has been changing. How she seems a little taller. There are curves to her now, and maybe there is something about those changes that make him want to touch her— and, isn't that what she had been wanting from Sebastian? For him to willingly reach out for her. Fingers to press into her with ease, and hold. She wants to sigh in tight embrace.

Mia takes a deep breath. Despite Daniel's stance, or his comments earlier about her teeth or the scars on her face, his scar creates a sense of vulnerability, a sense that in its obscurity, makes Mia feel like she has misunderstood him somehow. His words have centered a spotlight upon her. She is afraid of him, of the dark, of Benny in the shadows, and even of Sebastian's silence behind her, but she wonders now if this hidden place provides the kind of privacy she's long been curious about. She does not know what is worth exploring beyond touch, but the interest is bright in the tiny muscles of her body.

Mia, Daniel says.

His voice nicks the silence, her name flipping off his tongue. He reaches out his hand and tugs at the hem of her dress. She steps back, though not beyond his reach. His foot slides toward her, yanking the hem again, dress stretching over her bra.

Hey!

Mia jerks back, lifting momentum with her shoulders as she tips fluidly from his fingers.

Come on, Mia, isn't this what you wanted?

No.

Don't be dumb. Girls are always playing dumb, Daniel says.

Benny moves from kneeling to standing—his form a thing of disproportionate distance. He's there and he's not. And Sebastian, he is a memory:

when afternoons were very long, maybe two years ago. Sebastian flew on his skateboard down Indio Street and Mia sprinted behind him. Waxing scent to the air, blue blood of a dying cactus staining the breeze. The outlying mountains' translucent haze, early summer.

They were nine years old, going to one of two general stores in Marina Sal to buy Val cards for Mother's Day. She had given them five dollars each and they'd planned to buy ice cream with the remaining money.

When they entered the store, they were met with fans to ban flies. Scarce aisles offered Fritos, NesQuick containers a decade old, warm yellow Gatorade, batteries, bundles of sage, matches, strawberries from Brawley, and assorted candy bars both recent and years expired, among other random necessities.

Mia and Sebastian headed to the greeting cards. Some cards had been in the store since the 50s. Mia chose a card with painted roses on the cover. She knew Val wished to grow roses, but that the flower couldn't live through summers in Marina Sal.

They bought their cards and orange cream pops and stepped outside, the fans ushering the backs of their legs into the sun, and before Mia had a chance to open her popsicle, Sebastian handed her a card. It didn't have an envelope. A small brown puppy on the cover, and the puppy had large eyes. To Someone Nice, it said. She opened it. Everyone Should Be as Nice as You! The puppy was smiling with a small bird sitting on its head, big eyes directed toward its friend.

Sebastian looked at the ground, long arms swinging by his side. Kool-Aid stain on his oversized t-shirt. He had a scrape on his shin from running into Benny's bicycle while skateboarding.

Mia hadn't said anything for a long moment. She nodded, Thank you.

Sebastian nodded, and Mia shoved his shoulder and jumped off, sprinting toward the road home. And she heard his skateboard hit the concrete and she heard his laughter, his body gaining on her as he curved around and pushed ahead, yelling, Slow poke!

Sebastian is that Sebastian.

Mia turns, the memory warm in her chest, seeking him. Sebastian stands back, form stiff, and Daniel's hand is suddenly on her hip, and it's not a good touch, and her neck snaps forward, face to face with Daniel. He remains still as if waiting for her reaction.

She doesn't think about the movies now, about a woman's naked body, about whether or not she had misunderstood the boys, whether or not she is nice or they are nice, or the fact that Sebastian's body is close to her, their brief touching—she doesn't think about any of that, but her father comes to mind.

She stares Daniel straight in the eye. He looks at her the way her father looked at her when he told her anything at all: *You look like me, Mia.*

Let me teach you how to pray, Mia.

Stop crying, Mia.

I love you, Mia.

She draws her hand back—the tilt of her hips pulls a firmer grasp from Daniel—and she sees her father's red face, foreign and all too familiar, close above her eyes in the shadows.

Mia slaps him. She slaps Daniel hard.

This is an adventure, her father says, tongue hanging from his mouth as he pants.

Again, the final afternoon that Mia sees him. They leave the abandoned house, walk an empty street which brakes off at desert. They continue over hard dirt, eventually winding behind a wire fence lining the The Desert Oasis, a trailer park, where patches of Joshua trees reach needled fists toward the sky. Each trailer, sleek models from the '50s and '60s, erode. An old swing set creaks though there is no breeze.

Her father has a limp. He hops when swinging right foot in front of left, huffing each time his right hits the concrete. He's wearing worn flip-flops, scuffing gravel, mimicking his breathing. Mia takes small steps to keep in line with him.

Beyond the trailer park, they meet paved road again, lined still by Joshua trees, bodies conspicuous as the day's heat, painting alien shadows. Each element of the land sculpts a day-dream impression, generating the sense of levitation while rooted to the ground.

The two curve toward the south tip of the Salton Sea, walking in silence. Mia wants to go home, and she wonders if her mother is worried, or if her mother will come looking for her, and she hopes that her mother will, because she isn't sure how to leave her father.

Ropey legs hoist him forward, and his dry skin, old scabs spotting his ankles from desert brush, close to cracking. If she runs, he won't be able to catch her. But the way he breathes, the deep scuffs, causes Mia to hesitate. She feels sorry for him.

He needs help—that much she can understand.

The road rounds in, lining a tiny bay, where upon the shore a white couch and armchair are placed. Both pieces of furniture are soiled as if they'd been dipped in mud. Across the street from the sitting area is a deserted strip mall and liquor store. Every floor-to-ceiling window of the mall has been shattered, mirror-glass scattered across the parking lot, each piece reflecting the sky. On the side of the liquor store, the words HOW COULD A MAN PASS THIS BY? / I CAME IN PRAYING FOR YOU written in black paint. Beyond the strip mall, a billboard blank-white save for one statement written in gold spray paint: TURN OFF THE SUN.

Let's just stop for a sec', her father says.

He walks toward the couch and collapses on the cushions. Mia follows, but remains standing.

I like to come here to watch the sun rise, he says, before it gets too damn hot. I'm never the only one, neither. Lot of folks show to watch the sun come up. Gets me thinking about how nothing can't be too bad. The feeling don't last all that long, so I got to watch lots of sunrises to keep thinking it.

Mia stares at the sea's surface, sapphire like the mirror shards in the parking lot. Sand beneath her feet isn't sand, but an accumulation of finely crushed fish and bird bones. Squatting, she takes a handful. Staring at her cupped hands, she imagines a human's mouth wide and open, revealing serrated pink teeth.

A match rips and Mia blinks, shifting upon her heels. Hears the sound of flame flutter to life. Her father lighting a cigarette, cupping his hand and puffing. He tips his head back, shoots smoke into the air.

My God, that tastes better than rain.

Embers dance in loose circles. Her father coughs from deep within. Sunlight making the wounds on his forearms more pronounced—Mia sees red, wet holes in her father's skin, and bruises clouding the crook of his arm. He sucks in more smoke, holding it, releases curls from loose lips. Mia frowns. Bones light as water in her palm, and her hands begin to shake.

Ain't it hot? This place is hell on earth, he says.

Ur-an-us is the coldest planet, Mia says, watching the cigarette tilt in her father's hand. She touches the burn scar on her cheek. Scar flesh silky.

This is the hottest place in all the universe, I'd bet.

Ur-an-us is blue.

You already said it was blue.

Mia stands, dumping the bones back onto the shore. Down the road from the strip mall is an old public pool, which drained, now serves skateboarders. Mia can hear the bump of boards against concrete, muffled *Ahhs*, skidding rubber up pool walls. Before her the sea water is still, radiating torrid air. She shifts her weight because her feet hurt, but she doesn't want to sit beside him. He coughs again, body convulsing, and leans forward to spit.

That's where they went to die, he says.

Who?

My imaginary friends, he says. When you're older, you can't just get rid of people when you don't want them around no more. It ain't as easy as throwing someone away and never hearing from them again.

He sucks the end of smoke. Blue fans out, entering her pupils and mouth. Mia is dizzy. It doesn't seem to her that a person should want to throw someone away.

What? What you looking at—this? He lifts the cigarette to the sun. You wanna try it?

Heat pounds inside Mia's body. Trying to piece together her father and the day: a dead end road, jelly eyes, abandoned homes, wounds and blood. Bruises that look like the gases of space. Families they never were. A dirty couch, front seat to sunrise.

Mia isn't a part of any piece.

Bones beneath her feet crunching as she stamps her foot, and the sound is too loud. Teeth grinding. Tiny snaps of branches or firecrackers in memory, or bloody knuckles popping that time her father had punched a window after being angry with her mother, and he'd sat back at the kitchen table, laced his red, wet fingers, cracked them inward.

Mia shakes her head. She shakes it hard while a low moan grows from her, her mouth moving like it holds cotton. Tears come. Anger like this, so defined, is new to Mia. She hates her father. She hates this day, the sea, every color blazing around her.

He takes a final drag and dabs the cigarette into bones. He reaches out, gripping the back of her neck.

Be quiet, Mia, he says. Don't ruin our trip, you hear? What you cryin' for?

She can't speak, doesn't want to speak.

Shut up, Mia. Come on, you gotta be quiet. We're gonna go see Sebastian, okay? Shut up and we'll go see Sebastian.

Sebastian Sebastian Sebastian.

We'll go see Sebastian, and all of us will get some lunch. Just be quiet, will ya'?

Mia nods, cutting back a breath.

You gotta be quiet. Someone might think something is wrong.

Mia imagines Sebastian at home, watching TV on the couch or in Val's room. The fan on, slow circulations. Light floating through the back window. The hallway is always a tunnel of cool air and Mia loves to linger there, lie down, and sometimes Sebastian lies with her and they look for shapes in the textured paint splatters on the ceiling. All other rooms of the house silent, hours before Val returns from work.

Just a normal, long afternoon.

Mia and her father walk through desert, avoiding streets. Around them, textured fields of silver cacti and arrow weed stretch.

Her father releases her neck, but holds onto her shoulder, gripping tight as he directs her over the rough terrain. His hobbling lays strain to her back—she feels his nails dig into her skin, and she whines.

He jerks her head to his mouth, whispers, Shut up.

The sun beating. Breathing in and out, her steps forced in rhythm of his limp jarring her body. Panic rising inside of her, the earth popping in stillness, and her father spits, coughs, pushes her. His breathing angular behind her.

Eventually, the empty desert comes upon a neighborhood. An assortment of cement, short houses intermingled with trailer-homes. Her father slows his pace, scanning for other people. The street is clear as they approach the backyard gate to Val and Sebastian's house. The day's temperature, upwards of 100 degrees, keeping people indoors.

He stops Mia by the gate.

Don't make a fuss, you hear? I need you to go in there and get me some food. All that you can carry. You get that food and I'll go. Get me food and I'll go away from here for good.

She hears his words and sees his blistered lips move. Saliva swishing around in his mouth. Bottom row of teeth crooked, encrusted with yellow plaque. His pupils drawing in and out of focus.

She thinks about the scar on her face. Burning feeling a way she didn't know heat could feel. Ice. She wishes her father had never appeared in the abandoned house. She wishes this was a different man or that she was not real. A presence as memory morphing out of proportion, the way the recollection of flesh burning can't be fully realized, only becomes the remembrance of pain. She wants to scream, but her mouth won't open.

Mia opens the chain-link gate, and walks toward the sliding glass door. She will bring her father food, and he will leave. She will play games with Sebastian, or ride bikes, and maybe Val will allow her to stay for dinner. Maybe Val will make spaghetti, they will watch a movie, and maybe she will spend the night.

Inside, she hears white noise from the back bedroom. Sebastian is watching TV. She doesn't need to bother him. She can quickly bring her father the food, be done with it, and no one will know that she's stealing.

With quiet steps, she approaches the refrigerator and opens it. Her hands are shaking as she reaches for a pack of hot dogs and a half gallon of milk.

Mia?

Sebastian appears from behind the refrigerator. What are you doing? His hair is disheveled, and there is a red film on his teeth from candy.

Mia jumps, milk slipping from her hand. The carton smacking onto the floor.

My dad's outside, she whispers. He's hungry, and he wants me to bring him a lot of food.

Sebastian glares at the floor in thought, and then nods. He takes the hotdogs from her hand, grabs a loaf of bread and a bag of tortilla chips from the kitchen counter, and stuffs the groceries in a plastic bag.

On the patio, Sebastian says, Wait here.

He opens the fence, and Mia sees her father stand from where he had been sitting on the ground.

Is there more?

Sebastian shakes his head.

I know you got more.

Her father seizes Sebastian's arm and walks him toward the house. Mia wraps her arms around her body and backs away.

Come here, he says, grabbing her by a handful of hair. When she screams he yanks harder. The tug is shocking. Mia can hear Sebastian's breathing, straining through his nose. Her scalp pulled tight, her father takes them into the house and shuts the door.

Mia and Sebastian stand side by side next to the dining table. Their arms pressed together. His touch warm, and the moment, enumerated, plays out fixed, yet fluid. The urge to speak in a dream.

Her father scavenges the kitchen, stuffing lunch-size bags of chips, Twinkies, and fruit snacks in two plastic grocery bags he found in a drawer. He takes Val's half-empty bottle of Vodka and five or six RC Colas. He empties the cupboards, beading four bags onto one arm, keeping the other free. He moves through the kitchen with sharp deftness, as if he no longer has a limp. And then he pauses, looking at them, eyes suddenly sorry, and runs down the hall.

Sebastian chases after him.

Mia squats on the floor, covering her face with her hands. Rough carpet on her kneecaps, and she hears Sebastian's voice, small, hears a loud slapping sound, then several slaps in slow succession, eerie pauses. She's pressing her hands hard against her eyes. Her face pliable, wet.

Heavy footsteps come from the hall, slipping of his flip-flops, his body hauling, the limp reinstated, one step denser than the other, shopping bags sashaying against his sides.

Peering through her fingers, she catches sight of her father's figure. He's jerking the sliding glass door open.

He's disappearing into the sun.

A hot gust wafts into the room. Mia stands and watches her father shrink into the sand. She thinks of ants. She thinks of birds high in the sky, twisting elegantly. Shrinking things appear erratic, unlikely or shape-shifting. And she was relieved to see him wane to nothing, growing strange already in her mind. Each version of her father more distant as if he had been there yesterday, not minutes ago. As if he had been loving not in this lifetime, but the last.

When she closes the door, she hears silence more loudly than she's ever heard it.

Sebastian sits on the floor in Val's room. He's holding the side of his head and crying soundlessly. Val's velvet jewelry box is open on the floor, spare remaining contents—a ghost pin for Halloween, a dried carnation, orphan beads—splaying on the ground. Mia sits beside Sebastian, and lies her head on his shoulder. He smells like chili powder dusted on mangos. He sets his hand on top of her own. He exudes heat—the heat of his tears, the heat of his beating heart, of his fear and anger. The way his palm trembles over her hand, she knows the heat is for her.

Mia closes her eyes and imagines being held by no one in particular, just held against a body as in a tight hug. They stay like this for a long time, unable to determine how to break the silence, until Mia whispers, Sebastian, what are some things you like?

The tears have dried shiny on his face. He doesn't say anything for a long time.

I like watching TV, I guess.

What else? Tell me lots of things, like a grocery store list.

Okay…I like the windmills that I saw one time when mom and I were driving to L.A. My mom said they make electricity for us. I guess I like my mom. I like popsicles and I like hearing coyotes when it's night time. I like Spider-Man a lot.

He pauses, squeezing her hand.

And I love when it rains. Don't you think it's the nicest when it rains?

Mia and Sebastian, Daniel and Benny—the four stand with debris, where hotel guests once slept beneath a melon-colored serape, wiped Aloe Vera gel on burns. They stand in a room where couples touched limb to limb, transferring dried salt from their stomachs and backs. The couples who had floated in the Salton Sea's shallows.

The furniture removed, leaving empty rooms, white stucco walls covered in graffiti: poetry, child-like geometry. If it weren't so dark, they could see the words that are written, multicolored, lost in penumbra:

GOD IS LOVE.

GONE.

JULIETTE.

NATURAL HISTORY.

FUCK OFF.

NOTHING EVER HAPPENS.

Mia's hands press flat against her eyes—the slapping hand is supple and tingling. She has stepped away from Daniel, and he has stepped away from her. Mia blinks, tear drops flicking off her eyelashes, pooling in her hands. Maybe she has been holding her breath, or maybe she has forgotten how to breathe, but suddenly she scoops in air, mouth agape, like she is thirsty for it.

She drops her hands from her face. Daniel stands in spears of grey light. He's breathing hard. Lungs expand—his form bleeds into shapelessness. Lungs deflate—his form shrinks toward the grey. Mia's body feels balmy, filled with steaming water. Her limbs are what she hears right now. She doesn't hear Daniel's breathing. She doesn't hear Sebastian shuffling behind her. Doesn't hear Benny laughing at Daniel.

Mia hears her body quiver. Hears her blood shine.

Or maybe she hears the walls hum, the microscopic snaps in infrastructure. Each splinter giving way to years. Or outside coyotes sniffing around granite boulders, seeking gopher snakes, teeth snapping tiny bones.

Maybe the day isn't today, and maybe these things haven't happened. She wants the moment to be night, bedtime. She wants to slip into loose fitting clothes. Summers on the back-porch mattress.

And if this day is today, Daniel will react. A turn after the slap. Mia thinks that she must leave the Blue Palm. Leave the boys and their encroaching presence. Their hands which have touched her.

But Daniel's form, at first oscillating, hardens straight. He moves toward her without a sound.

/

Sebastian watches as Daniel moves toward Mia with arms outstretched. His palms collide with her chest, and Mia trips backward. At first she is a stiff board, but her body folds. Mia hitting the ground in a loose L-shape.

Sebastian's reaction is instantaneous, but splintered, his thoughts trace loss: he feels like he is missing something—an idea, a person. He's thirsty. He's tired. His pulse picks up. The future holds reprimanding. The future holds change. And his sense of loss does not just seem inescapable, loss itself becomes the sensation of inescapability. The way Mia's body folds, her arms swinging up over her head, her hair moving forward as she falls back—trapping Sebastian in the image. Her folding on loop behind his eyes. He entombed in her fragility.

It was like he had already hit Daniel.

Sebastian steps toward him feeling that he cannot lose. Just now, Sebastian lived it: he will step forward and his fingers will click into a fist, fingernails will leave small half-moons in his palm, and power will come from his shoulder blade. Wings climbing the wind. Impacting Daniel's face, shattering.

His body is inflexible. This fight is Sebastian's first. In the corner of his eye, Mia is crumbled, and within this glimpse, all of Mia is encased. She needs him. She needs his protection. A falling Mia plays and replays, folding, and then heat, muscles stitching with small explosions.

The urge to defend is luminescent, terrifying. Feels like watching a large animal exert beyond capacity. Hurling, rhythmic stride.

Or the urge is just that. The rhythm of terror to a child.

/

The broken tile on the floor of the abandoned hotel room reminds Mia of a specific cut of shoreline along the Salton Sea. At this location there is no beach. The sea had flooded, pewter water biting land, coating dirt in sulfur. Water skirts an old tennis court. After years of beating sun, base cement erosion, the green court began to crack. Mia imagined that the slabs, in some cases small enough to lift, were continents. She'd place a small slab in the shallow sea water, and inhabit the continent with seagull feathers, verbena flowers, paper fish skulls, apple snails. The sea encircling Mia's small land masses was more like soup, thick with insects, fish scales, and creamy mulch.

And that's what Mia thinks about, the broken tiles, the Salton Sea, and how the dead things putrefy in salt, become jelly. The dead magnified in her mind as she lies on the floor. Neon. Innards cooking in puckered water. Mia feels like she's been inside this hotel room for days. She feels like she hasn't slept in weeks.

And this is what dreamless sleep looks like: shadows at war, outer space viscous and littered with unknowns, faintly drawn possibilities, ghosts or a dramatic turn. Maybe she can close her eyes to awake elsewhere. Or, maybe Val will show up, break the boys apart, take her and Sebastian home. Or, maybe Mia's father will walk into the room, call out to the angel of death. If he had appeared out of thin air before, he could do it again.

Sebastian steps across her, shoves into Daniel. Their bodies collide. Mia listens to the boys breathe, concentrated exhales, groans. Fighting in dark mass. Benny rushing them, colliding.

At any moment, she'll wake up. She'll wake up on the patio, or in a different city, on a different continent, or an island, far out in the ocean.

The wind gestures westward. Palms bend toward the waves. Light transposes flocks of white birds onto the sound of Mia's own breathing.

She is far, far away.

Benny has one palm to Sebastian's chest and the other to Daniel's.

Fuck you man, fuck you, Daniel says. You a fucking a hero, huh? Daniel smacks Benny's arm, and recedes to the window. I can't breathe, he says. I can't breathe.

Daniel pulls on one of the boards nailed across the window. Nails squeak, give way, and Mia hears Daniel fall back, hears the sound of glass clank as if his body knocked some bottles. A glow spreads, a cloud of fresh light painting over the room.

The sun, the sun, the sun. Mia inhales.

I can't fucking breathe, Daniel says.

The dark diffused, Mia's vision adjusts. Benny stands tautly near Sebastian, blood smeared across his cheek. His eyes brim wet, expression withdrawn. Sebastian's arms hang in front of him, lax and curved. His chest heaves. The room is in worse condition than she had imagined. Rubble making small mountains. Broken skateboards, blackened strips of insulation, drywall, small desert rocks stacked like columns, pages from newspapers, magazines, comic books, soiled paperback novels, smashed paper cups, pieces of glass. She scans all of the corners, looking for her father amongst the ruin.

But she finds Daniel again who has been quiet. He's looking through the window's gap. Bleached light, drowsy flies. He steps back and his foot bumps a glass bottle again, turns toward Sebastian, who stands only feet from Mia.

You're a pussy, Daniel says.

His eyes are bright red. He picks up one of the bottles. It's an empty, voluptuous liquor bottle, glass foggy from age. It takes him only three steps to reach Sebastian. Daniel grips the bottle high above his head, and the streak of light catches in the glass, fills it. The two or three seconds suck into the dark as Mia shuts her eyes.

Is she standing? She stands, maybe, legs made of old wood it seems. Scrapes on her knees sting. But she's on the floor, still, too.

She's both. In her mind she has stood and she has pushed Sebastian out of Daniel's path.

/

Though Daniel moves toward him, Sebastian doesn't move.

Energy, once vexed hot in his muscle, now feels thirsty. The adrenaline has run out.

To Sebastian, Daniel is no longer his friend. Daniel is not the boy who rides bikes with him, siphons ants into jars using bendy straws, collects baseball cards, who skates with self-reliance. He is not the Daniel who says that when he is old enough, he wants to get a dog, marry a nice girl, own a home. Daniel, who misses his dead brother. Who dreams about his brother visiting him at school—just showing up and taking him from class and driving away, to no destination in particular. This Daniel is not that Daniel.

Sebastian is sick of the trash, the acrid scent, the way his lungs seem to say *We don't want to breathe anymore.*

Maybe that's what Daniel meant, too?

I can't breathe, Sebastian thinks. I don't want to breathe like this.

Daniel smashes the bottle across Sebastian's shoulders. Center splitting. The neck remaining clutched in Daniel's hand. The sound is a thud, and cascading, shards echoing like beads scattering.

Sebastian kneels beside Mia, and she can see his face screwed tight. His breath and his voice contained. He traps something inside of himself. He doesn't come loose, not again. He collects, packs every part close and closer and he lays his forehead on his bended knee.

Blood drips from his neck.

He's so close to her. His trembling form. Collecting, tightening, closer and closer he draws in, brushing her naked calf.

Daniel is the doctor. Mia the patient, and Sebastian is her father.

I will see you now, Daniel says. They follow him into his backyard shed.

Come on, sweetie, Sebastian says to Mia, and she takes his hand.

Mia holds her stomach with her other hand, pretending that it aches. They are five years old.

Inside the shed is a single dangling light bulb cocooned by cobwebs. Sunlight falling through a bluish spider web that stretches across a single window. Daniel's father keeps the lawnmower, weed wacker, and a couple jugs of insecticide in the corners. Otherwise, the space provides ample room to play, Daniel's favorite place to be while at home. He's decorated the walls with artifacts discovered from abandoned buildings or fields—a horseshoe, a soiled Scooby Doo stuffed toy, coins from the '50s, a newspaper clip of an eclipse, a beheaded G.I. Joe with chew marks on its thighs.

Daniel likes to play in the shed because it feels like a house of his own, a house separate from his parents' home only a couple hundred feet across the brown yard. Inside his parents' house, his father drinks gin and root beer, mouth numbing and the liquid pooling around his teeth; and inside that house his brother bruises his arms, words hot on his ear, *pussy shit, worthless bitch*; and inside that house, his mother whispers and knits, never dusts, weight gain cramping her legs. She sleeps full afternoons, neck snapped across the couch arm.

Every opportunity that Daniel has, he plays in the shed. He has different imaginary games he alternates—lately, he's a doctor working in what he imagines New York City to be like. This fantasy came about through Daniel's uncle, a man who had always been kind to Daniel. His uncle brought him Tootsie Rolls every Christmas, taught him how to tie his shoes, once smacked Daniel's brother across the face after his brother punched him.

He once had told Daniel that he has a great imagination.

The uncle had lived in New York City for five years when he was in his mid-thirties, and had told Daniel about a particular New Year's Eve. He was visiting his friend, a woman who lived in a high rise smack in the middle of the island. From her windows, you could see every neighborhood stretching in each direction. At midnight there were fireworks from several different neighborhoods, so many that the night sky was a complete shade of bright yellow.

And Daniel loved that image: large sky over skyscrapers, volume tilting the North American continent, night sky bright as dawn.

One afternoon, the phone rang and his mother answered—she mumbled tightly into the receiver, her voice shaped to a needle point. Daniel strained to hear. Her voice dropped mid-sentence into heavy pause, and then she hung up the phone with slow precision. His mother walked into the kitchen and whispered to his father. This time, Daniel could overhear every word—his uncle had died from a heart attack. His mother once told him that dreams happen only as a person is waking: entire episodes of thought taking place in mere seconds. He learned that though things can happen very fast, so much is still felt. When he heard the news, he thought he could be waking from a nightmare.

Daniel waited days for his mother to tell him, too. The longer she went without bringing it up, the more Daniel believed he had misheard. But months, years passed. His uncle never returned to visit.

Daniel will never see his uncle again. He understands too, that his uncle will never see fireworks again.

After the passing, Daniel began to pretend that he was a doctor. He became the doctor who saved his uncle's life. He imagined living in an exciting place. Imagined helping sick people. And so when Sebastian wanted to play and he asked to bring Mia, Daniel was happy to have someone to play the patient.

Come in! Daniel holds the door open for Sebastian and Mia. He's set up a plastic lawn chair as an examination table.

Sit here, Mia. What's wrong?

My tummy hurts, Mia says.

Does it hurt bad? Daniel asks Sebastian.

Sebastian perks up. Yeah, I think real bad, he says.

Mia giggles. Daddy let me eat too much candy, she says.

Let me check your heart.

Daniel touches Mia's chest. He doesn't pretend to listen for her heart; he actually searches for the beat. Hand resting until her movement enters his hand, pulsing gently into his own blood.

Can I listen to it? Daniel says.

What?

Your heart.

Okay.

Mia looks over at Sebastian picking his nose. Gross! She laughs as Daniel presses his ear against her chest, and he hears her laughter reverberate inside. She smells like milk, a sweet floral waking late. Daniel finds that he loves the scent.

Sebastian looks ashamed, which only stirs more laughter, filling her, moving against Daniel's face. When her laughter dies away the heartbeat emerges. Sonorous, the sound of falling asleep. Daniel's thoughts swinging between the memory of his uncle and an image of a heart floating inside the body.

I hear it! Daniel says.

What does it sound like? Mia asks.

Like a drum.

I wanna hear, Sebastian says. He moves from the corner. Both boys pressing their ears against her chest.

Boom, boom, boom, Mia says. She begins to laugh again, and Sebastian says Whoa, which Daniel knows to mean Sebastian can hear the laughter too, and the boys smile, catch the urge, fall onto Mia in their own amusement.

The three sprawled on the floor, sunlight a big block across their legs.

And years move forward. Spider webs replacing older spider webs, threads thickening. Daniel's brother shoots himself in the shed. This, the dream: both his brother and uncle will show up at school, take Daniel from class, and they will drive away in a convertible, and they will never stop driving. They will see large cities. They will see new people. The car will move fast enough that Daniel will see the range of the world, but never grow attached to it. He'll lean back in the sun. He'll feel the breeze, air wreathed with physical embrace.

Sebastian hunches, blood shiny on his tanned neck. He shakes like a small animal. Mia thinks of the time she held a baby starling, fallen from a nest stitched into a Joshua tree. Yarn weaving twigs and human hair. Wind shook the clouds and pine. The tiny creature fell from the nest, featherless. Skin translucent lavender. The bird trembling in her palm.

Mia considers the scale of things. A baby bird she once held in her hand to the muscle in hands, muscle which can squeeze, or speak or count minutes, seconds.

The size of cities Mia has never seen. The size of oceans and depths in the earth which will always remain a place in her head. Her imagination is only so big. Layers and layers and time, hours, weeks, years. All ideas grow. Most objects, most people, have limits.

Stop screaming, Benny says. His hand is on Mia's shoulder. She didn't know he was so close to her.

She has dreamt of being Sebastian's wife one day. How could it be any other way? Mia has only ever imagined that her life will converge with Sebastian's permanently, that she will always sleep beside him and wash his cereal bowl in the mornings and ask him what he likes and doesn't like, and he will touch her gently. He will care about whether or not she is happy.

She steadies her breath. Benny standing behind her, hand remaining on her shoulder. All four are quiet. The room sings the imagery of comatose.

And then a creak at the door. Mia turns her head, and she sees a man standing in the doorway.

He makes a hissing movement—his breathing raspy, steam losing tension through a clogged spout. He hovers in the doorway.

The man is nonsensical, an enigmatic altercation in their stillness, the stillness that had, for several minutes, erased Mia's screams and Sebastian's shaking and Benny's touch and Daniel's quiet tears.

The man is a time traveler inching toward the center of the room.

I heard screaming, the man says. Which one of you was screaming so goddamned loud?

The man's voice unfolds splinter by splinter. Breaks between words. Cough huge in his throat.

Mia, still sitting on the floor, is nearest the man as he walks closer. She can smell his body. Metallic. Dark urine. Mia thinks that the man must be close to dying. She has never seen a dead person. With each shift of his leg, his heaviness glistens in the cloud of sun. It's not her father, she knows, but he could have been. The man's face is not her father's face. His tattoos, eyes, body shape are of another man's.

This man is round. His shirtless stomach streaked with dirt. He's barefoot, and his toes appear caked with tar. Pale skin sunburnt. Bleached hair is cut jaggedly, shaved along the sides, and pieced apart by grease. His beard falls thinly from his face, accumulating to a pointed tip near his belly button.

You all are babies, the man says.

Mia leans back an inch, not wanting to be the thing he focuses on. She remembers that there are other people in the hotel. She had forgotten about them, or the idea of them.

Had she wanted the man to be her father? The idea summons tears, but she fights back. Had it been him, he wouldn't have helped her. He wouldn't have helped Sebastian. She squeezes her own legs, and the energy won't drain. She digs her nails into her own flesh, and the digging hurts, but doesn't hurt enough, wanting the ones who hurt us. If he was somewhere out in the world, why couldn't that somewhere be the Blue Palm? The vast structure, room after room of hidden bodies in refuge.

Sebastian stands. Blood from his neck wound has managed to leak beneath his shirt, run across his shoulder and down his arms. The other boys are stiff in place.

Sorry we bothered you, sir, Sebastian says.

You sure did, son. What was you yelling for? There's folks sleeping in the hotel, don't you know?

The man scans their faces closely. Grumbling, he nods, wiping sweat from his brow. What are you doing up here? It's dangerous. You live here?

No, no, we were just messing around, Sebastian says.

Son, you're bleeding, the man says.

He walks toward Sebastian. When the man passes Mia, she can see the folds of his skin lined by dirt. He has a hobble like her father did, and the way his breathing gushes through his nose when he walks brings her to feel concerned for him.

What the hell is going on. Miss, you the one yelling?

His eyes fasten to Mia. Yellow surrounds the irises, and his eyelids are blood red. The man appears concerned the way Val would look if she were here. Val would gather Mia and Sebastian into her arms. Mia would press her face into Val's neck, and Sebastian's face so close to hers, his breath against Mia's cheek. Val would smell like the house, like cooking breakfast or dust in a potpourri pot.

The man grabs onto Sebastian's shoulder and moves his eyes from Mia to look at the wound on Sebastian's neck, tilting Sebastian's body down at an angle.

Was it you, little miss? He asks again.

Was what me? Mia says.

She presses her nails deeper into her thigh. Deep as the nails will go. Half moons. Her legs are sticky.

Were you hollering?

I guess that was me, but I don't remember.

How is it you don't remember? You were screaming bloody murder for Christ's sake.

Mia remembers and she doesn't. She remembers the glass breaking across Sebastian, and fear moving her breath, and maybe, Yes, she can hear her own cry and her own echo. Or she can feel Benny's hand on her shoulder. Or Sebastian's shaking form, crouched and balled. The board being stripped. Daniel's hand on her hip. Her father. It all happened moments ago.

Little girl, was that you hollering? Were these boys hurting you? The man continues to hold Sebastian's arm. Daniel and Benny have slackened their posture, though remain frozen in place. Did this boy hurt you, huh? You fight back? That why he bleeding? He jostles Sebastian. Answer me!

Sebastian is limp in the man's hand, and his body twists back and forth in sharp turns. To Mia, Sebastian looks younger in the man's grip, like he is five years old. Sebastian whispers that he is dizzy.

Mia doesn't like the way Sebastian is a doll loose in the man's hand. A doll you could take apart, limb by limb. She doesn't like the way he appears weak, and half of her wants to scream again, yell as loud as she can and dig in as far as she can, and she wants to squeeze herself, feel physical pressure, open, peel, throw herself.

She's tired. Very tired.

Mia wants to go home, sink into sleep beside a Sebastian that isn't a doll, isn't bleeding. Why had he allowed her to come to the hotel? Had he known what Daniel would do? Mia wasn't sure what would have occurred had she not slapped Daniel, but she understood the action would have been harmful, because suddenly there seemed to be something harmful about the touching Mia saw on the TV screen, butter-light and all, people grabbing each other the way she wanted to grip through her own legs. Taking apart limb by limb. Throwing. Pushing.

Maybe it wasn't a beautiful thing, sex. Maybe it wasn't beautiful at all, and maybe Sebastian had known that, and had taken her, regardless, to the Blue Palm.

The room shrinks. Collage of shadow, garbage, a searing sun closes in on her body. She is naked in her mind, reflected in the bathroom mirror, her new softness, her curves, and she hates it. She hates the way she connects, and she hates her teeth, the pockets of fat, the sensitive spark in her belly, inner thighs. She hates the dull shade of her hair. The roundness of her face. She hates every person in the room.

One day, the ocean. Fields of flowers. An artist paints midnight. Forests just as big. Cities just as dark and rolling and open.

I ain't pulling no teeth, the man says. You answer me or else your friend is gonna get it.

I remember. Yes, it was me screaming.

Her voice is hard the way Daniel had been talking to her earlier. She speaks with conviction, straight-forward, an engraving tone as if to say Yes, I will always remember that I was the one screaming.

Alright then. Were the boys hurting you, little girl?

The man jerks Sebastian, and with his free hand, he points at Daniel and Benny.

One day.

Yes, Mia says. They were hurting me.

The man lines the boys up against the wall.

Air on Sebastian's neck wound stings. Though several minutes have passed, Sebastian still feels light-headed from the bottle's impact, and his stomach distends like he'll be sick. He perceives his back is against a wall, and that Benny stands to his left, Daniel to his right. Across from them, Mia stands next to the man. Her head reaches just below his armpit, and his forearm drapes across her shoulder. But Sebastian is still coming to terms with his body's heaviness, the nausea swinging through him. He bends forward, arms wrapping around his own waist. His upper back tightening when he breathes too deeply. Beside him, Daniel and Benny are motionless, arms straight at their sides.

Bunch of damn fools. Look at this pretty little girl. You think you're grown-ass men or what?

Sweat sliding down Sebastian's face. He wants the room to stop spinning, to grip a point of focus, but all the light, the shadows, slip from him and smear.

I had a daughter, the man says. I had a beautiful daughter. If anyone hurt her, I would kill 'em.

He squeezes Mia's shoulder.

Little girls are god's best gift to earth. They the closest thing to angels. He pauses, looks at Daniel. Hey! Pay attention, he shouts.

Sebastian shivers.

I had me a little girl as pretty as this one. What's your name, sweetheart?

Mia whispers.

What was it? Speak up, damn-it.

Mia.

I had me a daughter as pretty as Mia. When she was born, I thought there could be nothing more holy than that. Nothing on earth. But, I can't even say her name out loud to you all now—no, I can't. Can't say her name, 'cuz she too good, and I'm not good. My princess, though. She was my princess.

The man clears his throat, moves Mia closer to his body. Sebastian catches Mia's eye. Her eyes in focus until the dizziness slides his vision, but he tries to crawl back to her gaze.

He squeezes the image: her expression blank. The man's fingers spider-out across her bare shoulder. He wonders why she stands so near to the man. Is she looking at Sebastian? She seems to look beyond him. Looking into the wall, or into her mind. Sebastian tightens his knees, heaves his chest up to stand straighter.

I ain't no good, the man says. Lost all I had, job, daughter, wife, house. Why some things never come back, that's a question that's hard.

The man sways, and Mia's body, leaning into his, sways too. Sebastian feels sicker than ever, but alert after noting Mia's expression, her form lax against a stranger. She's acting like the man knows her and she knows him. The man's deep slur, his coarse voice wavering, and the man's eyes trembling in their sockets. The man isn't well.

Bile inches in Sebastian's throat. He wants to fix it, fix everything. Fix Daniel, Mia, the man, himself. Nobody is who he thought they were.

Mia, Sebastian says. Mia, what are you doing?

Don't talk to her! The man says.

Sebastian searches her face, but she offers no sign to him. What is she thinking? Saliva gathering in Sebastian's mouth, and his stomach churning. Nausea rendering his arms numb.

Mia—

I said don't fucking talk to her! She don't deserve the likes of you. She too good, can't you see that? Little girl, which one of them hurt you? I'd kill a man for touching my daughter.

The man strokes Mia's hair with the hand not clutching her shoulder. Each pet is heavier than the last. Mia begins arcing her neck to the side, attempting to slouch away from his touch. Though still distant, Mia's expression now reveals concern. Her mouth tightens.

Stop, Sebastian says. Can't you see she doesn't like you touching her like that?

Daniel and Benny whisper to each other, but Sebastian can't hear what they're saying. He takes a step toward the man, breathing through his nose, saying, Stop, stop touching her like that.

But his efforts don't matter. The man shoves Mia to the side, and she trips to the floor. His other arm swings in from Sebastian's blurred periphery, and the hand seizes Sebastian's skull, thumb pressing into his jaw. Sebastian is shunted, then pushed back against the wall, and the quick impact sparks nausea once and for all.

Release. Sebastian buckling over and heaving. Ribs constricting hard. His brain is either shrinking or expanding. He loses his balance. Sebastian falls, head landing on plaster chips and tile. Daniel and Benny run from the room. The man shouts, but doesn't pursue them.

Mia limp on the floor. Sebastian sees her thigh, her leg curving into a pair of white cotton underwear. When she fell, her skirt flew up.

The man shouting at the empty doorway. Sebastian watching Mia's leg. Tracing over and over the line from knee to lower back. Soft arc. Smooth skin. He waits for her to move, to resituate her dress. He waits, and for a brief instant, Sebastian wonders if she is even alive.

The necessity to stand rages. He lifts with the same urgency which sent him rushing toward Daniel earlier.

But as he stands, he's knocked down again. The man's face enlarges. The man's hand finds Sebastian once again with cold impact. The sound is like sprinting.

Her shoulders slip with his oils. He smells like metal. A pungent, acerbic metal—vapors rich in his pours. Monkey bars. Empty playgrounds. The sea.

She reaches for the day she found her father in the abandoned house. Hadn't her father smelled the same way? Oxidized. The dead parts of the Salton Sea. Featherless wings, spines, marbled joints and marrow, dehydrated eyes cemented into yellow-crusted mud.

She doesn't move from the man's side because he's so unsteady, as her father had been. And she's afraid to upset him. The man speaks to the boys, voice sloshing in his mouth, and Mia thinks about the man's daughter. She wonders what the little girl looks like, and if she looks anything like her. Is she Mia's age? Maybe his daughter is younger, with blonde hair like her father's, with the same blue eyes. Mia imagines that the girl hates her father. The girl will grow up and pretend he never happened and it will be easy to pretend.

The inside of the man is dead. A breaking-down has begun, and his organs, muscles, are already decomposing, releasing fumes. Mia thinks about how this man will one day never have happened. He'll be gone. What can't be seen. Disappeared into the earth.

Mia's mind, with all of these thoughts, feels numb.

Then the man is pushing her to the ground. When she looks up, he's clutching Sebastian's head. He steers his body against the wall, slamming him. At impact, Sebastian doubles over and coughs, face straining.

Mia shields her face in her bent arm. She is splayed across gravel bits of wall and tile, and she feels her dress hiked above her underwear, but she doesn't care. I don't care, I don't care, I don't care. Silently, she repeats the words into her own skin.

You ever touch another little girl again I will kill you. You hear me? I will kill you.

The man's voice is small now. He slaps Sebastian. Slaps him again.

And with the sound, Mia is everywhere. Her head is on Sebastian's shoulder. She's sleeping between her parents. She's the night. She's staring at the sky and it's a dome and there is hope that the ceiling will be lifted, something more real exists after space, and life is shaping itself in that hope. She finds herself, a feeling that is everywhere and possible, in each piece that she has continuously collected in her hands: the colors of time, love for a body, destiny in other people, earth imitating a dark imagination. Everywhere there is no death, no cruel act. In no part of herself does she find violence, but she must take what she wants.

Mia no longer wants to wonder why Sebastian brought her to the Blue Palm, and why he led her into that very room, allowed Daniel to act. She doesn't consider the things which make her feel ashamed, or embarrassed for having trusted Sebastian. In an instant, she is up on her feet, and she spots a rusted piece of rebar protruding from a pile of drywall.

First, Mia hits the man behind his kneecap. Strikes the rebar against tendon.

Then her arms swing the metal rod across his back. Here, he twists. But she strikes his gut, and the man's knees hit the floor, hands forming an X across his stomach.

Princess, what are you doing?

The man's eyes are so full of tears that there is no white surrounding the iris: drops obscure, act as a magnifying glass, and the entirety of both his eyes burn blue. Mia halts for only a moment. She's the man's daughter. Or wishes the man were her father. Or Mia wishes that she had hit her own father, and she drops the bar, and moves toward Sebastian, grabs his hand. It's okay, Sebastian, stand up, stand for me, good, come with me.

They run from the room and down the hall of the Blue Palm. Sebastian coughs, mining his lungs. He moves slower than Mia, but her adrenaline will not allow him to falter. She grips his hand and pulls him forward. They slide into the foyer: an emerald pool, or swamp, vaporous with still life. Mia directs them to the window from which they first entered. Daylight seeps from boarded slits, and as she nears the window, Mia can see the desert, and she can see the road. She can see the Salton Sea. A platinum strip, mute.

iii

—pushing through gauze. She's wound; she cannot move her legs.

Sheet wrapped tightly around their bodies, the scent of inner elbows. Sebastian whimpering in his sleep. Sheet balled tight in his hand. He's jerking and twisting enough to collect Mia and tie her to him.

Up and up her mind pulling, until her eyes open to night. She's tucked into Sebastian—arm pasted to ribs, knees aligned and bent in unison. She pushes her hand against his back, and she feels his muscles flexing.

Sebastian, she whispers.

She presses his shoulder toward her, rolling him onto his back. Loosening the sheets around his body, she lies her hand on his chest. Heartbeat in hand.

His eyes fling open and stare at her, taking her in. He wraps his arms around her.

I had a nightmare, he says. My mom and me were in the car. And we drove until mom was headed for a wall. I couldn't say a word. She just didn't seem to notice that she was going right for the wall. And when we hit, everything went black. I felt myself getting smaller and smaller. All the words I had wanted to shout just kind of got smaller. I couldn't move. I had nothing to move. I was just nothing, and I can't even explain that. I was nothing.

Sebastian speaks into Mia's shoulder, into her hair. After some time, she allows her body to relax into their embrace, her weight alleviating into him, and her chest rests upon his.

He's a child, Mia thinks. She's stroking his forehead.

The two lay in silence for a long time. Mia listens to Sebastian breathe into sleep—the breaths continually deeper, a rhythm both mechanical and organic. She loves to listen to him fall asleep, feel the slight contractions of his thighs, or a vulnerable moan, thoughtless as he drifts. The mammoth dark settles into her too, and her body eases into, then seems to merge with, the mattress. She sinks into semi-consciousness.

She feels like a flower closing its petals. She feels like a deflating balloon.

Sleep half-summer, half-celestial, timeless.

Sebastian is space. Sebastian is an island. Sebastian is every color.

．

She is a landscape which holds small lives. She is uncharted depths, prayers. Places she has never been; things she will never see.

She is outlined by the day. Mia touches her hips and collar and sternum and the top tip of her spine. And how can hours feel like days. And how do we pretend they are not.

.

The Blue Palm is miles from home, but only a short distance from a cluster of abandoned houses, the ones trimmed in arrow weed and cacti. The sub-division is perched along a slight ravine, and so lifted feet from the valley floor, receives the sun's beating in the late afternoon. At this hour, the homes, covered in graffiti, stripped to shambles, glow. Mia and Sebastian run through Marina Sal, though the man doesn't chase them. They run with speed that lifts their feet, pulling into dangerous momentum. And Mia pushes more, stretching her legs to the point of anguish. Her thighs rub. Her chest is bound to her back bones.

They pass the sunrise couch where once Mia had stood along the shore while her father smoked a cigarette. The glass shards once spread through the strip mall parking lot are now dust, and the billboard which now reads: TOO MANY HUMANS in rounded letters and purple paint. They run past the trailer park, the broken swing-set, the Joshua trees, and they keep running until they enter the abandoned neighborhood.

The two approach the house, perfectly square, painted the same mint green color. The date palm is there, still exuding the scent of warm sugar, but the house no longer appears as a home. The paint has dulled and each window is shattered. The lawn has turned brown and scarce, leaving yawning holes of dirt. Rubble, cans, crumbled papers create fringe.

Where are we? Sebastian holds his cramping side.

Mia's chest heaving. Perspiration feathering every pocket of her form. She feels stretchy as she breathes and breathes, hands on hips, squeezing her own bone.

She says, We're home.

Mia walks into the house through a doorless frame. She isn't worried that Sebastian will follow; she knows that he will.

Inside, garbage from outdoors continues across the floor. In what used to be the living room, a wall is completely stripped of plaster and sheetrock, exposing rusted pipes. The carpet has been removed, revealing patches of foam padding and concrete. The furniture is stained with the sweat of every person who had found shelter there, including her own father. The sweat marks marble the cream couch brown. Ripples of lives.

Mia has not been inside this house since she saw her father emerge from its hallway nearly six years ago. The house is no longer a newly abandoned entity, fresh with clues of domestic habitation. The space is now hollow. Within its walls, not a single memory of a family unit remains, save for the original architecture. The house has kept its skeleton, its layout which ruminates suburbia: a three bedroom, two bath family home with a spacious back yard, and what's more, a patio with a BBQ pit. The front yard overlooks a dip in the Sonoran Valley, and the Salton Sea, from your window, is at its stillest—do you see? Serenity.

Mia senses spatial recollection. She moves to the center of the living room, just as she had done when she was six years old. She had pretended to have a family. Her daughter's name was Sandra. Her husband had always been Sebastian.

He breathes.

Mia listens.

Her eyes focus on the graffiti. Questions climb across the walls, thick and multi-veined like old vines. Every shade of spray paint imaginable, every style or script.

CAN I TRUST WHAT I WANT?

WHY CAN'T I BE BETTER?

IS GOD REAL?

WHAT IS UNIVERSAL?

WHY DID I LET HIM HIT ME?

WHY DID MY MOTHER STAY?

TELL ME HOW TO MAKE IT EASIER?

CAN I START OVER?

AM I WHAT YOU WANTED?

WILL YOU WANT ME ONE DAY?

HOW WILL I DIE?

DID YOU FORGET ALREADY?
WHY DO PEOPLE LIE?
WHO WILL HELP ME?
WHO WILL MISS ME?
WHAT'S THE DEEPEST SECRET YOU KEEP?
PROMISE THAT YOU WON'T CHANGE, EVEN IN MY MEMORY?

And the words curve into shadows, drip onto the floor, spill onto the backyard concrete. Question marks erratic, a still drift down the walls like a photo of rain.

Mia follows the questions into the kitchen, and after standing for a period of time, she sits cross-legged, back resting against the broken refrigerator. Pictures of the home's former owners have been taken away. The table is gone. Orange linoleum peels. There is a melon-sized hole waist high in the wall across from her, and through the hole, she sees a spear of sunlight catching dust revolutions in another room. The light captures her, and she stares as it fades to a rose shade.

She doesn't think about the man or the Blue Palm. She doesn't think about Daniel or Benny. Sebastian stands to her left. Blood now makes scales on his neck. He doesn't lower his body beside her, but leans against the wall and stares into his own silence. In that moment, Mia doesn't care where Sebastian's gaze is focused. She stares at her own time-continuum: fading light in a forgotten house, an expired day, numb hour, powdered nerves, and forever a desert transposed on space or vice versa. And she's thinking about her parents, mostly her father. Senses dulling, her mind disconnecting from her body.

She does not feel her curves, does not feel the sunburn tightening her forehead, does not register her own breathing. She wonders if her father still wanders from empty home to empty home.

Maybe he turned his life around. Maybe he married another woman. Maybe he lives in Los Angeles, or maybe he moved to a different country, found himself a home in the shade of coastal trees. Or maybe her father was on that plane, the one from the news report that morning. Maybe he was traveling to Australia, and at once suspended, the plane dove, descending into the Pacific. Maybe the cabin filled with cold water, and maybe, as he prepared to hold his breath, he thought about the bluest planet in space. The thought coming to him suddenly, lakes of diamond, a planet of dense clouds spinning in the dark. Maybe he found her voice in the weight of sinking.

His trace is the heat scrawled on the horizon, a kind of luminescent echo. Desert stretches backward, ever inked by the sun's various colored light.

Mia knows that her father is dead.

Sebastian sits near her; their breathing rises and falls nearly in sync.

I'm sorry, Mia.

His sweat is pearly, and he licks his lips. His back is arched forward, collecting his belly into a small mound beneath his shirt.

She wants to unstick a stray hair from his forehead. She wants to hold his hand. Her mind and body disconnecting again, but this time it's her body which leads, and she stands from the floor.

Sit here, she says, pointing to where she had been sitting. He slides his body over and leans against the refrigerator.

Look through that hole. Don't stop looking through it, she says. Promise?

He nods. She turns and walks into the other room, closing the door behind her. She looks through the hole at Sebastian. Backing away, she keeps her eyes on him, holding his gaze. When she reaches the back wall, she stands straight.

Can you see me? She asks.

I can see most of you, he says.

Turning her back from him, she draws in a deep breath. She lifts her dress over her body, discarding it to the floor. Then the bra. Her heart pounding beneath her breasts. Her pulse is a current, and the air acts like a switch turning on her body, igniting goose bumps to rise up her legs and arms, and the light is palpable, hazel, and sweat on her back exhales. Mia stands in her underwear, and she shivers— a quick, violent twitch. Glancing over her shoulder, she turns.

From where she stands, she can see his neck down to his hands which rest in his lap. His fists are clamped tightly. From across the room and through the hole she can see the white of his knuckles. And when she bows her face downward, she finds his chin, his cheeks, and the tears in his eyes.

Mia's ache, the chemical vulnerability, has an eternity of its own. Minerals lace evening air. She can hear him looking at her.

She closes her eyes for a beat, and another, and she isn't there anymore. She isn't anywhere at all.

ACKNOWLEDGEMENTS

Endless gratitude to Garrett Dennert and Orson's Publishing for believing in this project. To Garrett—you are the most generous and considerate editor, and I thank you for your remarkable support, keen eye, and unparalleled kindness. I'm beyond lucky to have worked with you. Thank you, thank you, thank you.

To my parents and Cole: thank you for shaping my world. Thank you for sharing your creativity with me. Thank you for the many adventures, the many laughs. For being big-hearted. For being open-minded. For being brave. And for the encouragement and love, I owe you everything. With all my heart, thank you for being who you are.

To other family and precious friends, I'm sincerely grateful for your extraordinary presence in my life. I couldn't have reached this point without learning from your authenticity, your gentleness, and your powerful ambitions. Thank you for reading or commenting on this work, listening to me talk about it, or offering emotional support during its journey. Thank you for believing in me—a gift I appreciate more than I know how to say.

To Junse Kim, Andrew Joron, and Carolina de Robertis: this project would not have seen an end without your influence. Thank you for your art, your beautiful minds, and the support. I will remember your teaching for the rest of my life.

And to Fisayo, my home, my hero: your imagination, perspective, and love are the greatest treasures I will ever know. Thank you for every single moment you guided me onward. Thank you for being such a strong light.

ABOUT KAYLA EASON

Kayla Eason was raised in Angels Camp, a small town in the rural foothills of Northern California. Her writing has long explored unassuming pockets of the world, and the eclipsed inhabitants tucked therein. Place, nature, and wild silence often rule her imagination.

In 2017, she earned an MFA in Fiction from San Francisco State University, where she taught undergraduate courses first as a graduate teaching assistant and then lecturer. In the past, she's been an arts journalist and jewelry designer. Alongside writing, she pursues film photography. Her work has appeared in various literary publications.

Kayla currently lives in Southern California. You can read her other writing and check out her visual work at kaylaeason.com.

9 781733 817110